EDEN REBELLION

ABI FALASE

1

BBC Books, an imprint of Ebury Publishing
20 Vauxhall Bridge Road,
London SW1V 2SA

BBC Books is part of the Penguin Random House group of companies whose addresses can be found at global.penguinrandomhouse.com

Novel copyright © Abi Falase 2024

Abi Falase has asserted their right to be identified as the author of this Work in accordance with the Copyright, Designs and Patents Act 1988

No part of this book may be used or reproduced in any manner for the purpose of training artificial intelligence technologies or systems. In accordance with Article 4(3) of the DSM Directive 2019/790, Penguin Random House expressly reserves this work from the text and data mining exception

Doctor Who is produced in Wales by Bad Wolf with BBC Studios Productions. Executive Producers: Jane Tranter, Julie Gardner, Joel Collins, Phil Collinson and Russell T Davies

First published by BBC Books in 2024

www.penguin.co.uk

A CIP catalogue record for this book is available from the British Library

ISBN 9781785949197

Editorial Director: Albert DePetrillo
Project Editor: Steve Cole
Cover Design: Lee Binding
Typeset by Rocket Editorial Ltd

Printed and bound in Great Britain by Clays Ltd, Elcograf S.p.A.

The authorised representative in the EEA is Penguin Random House Ireland, Morrison Chambers, 32 Nassau Street, Dublin D02 YH68

 Penguin Random House is committed to a sustainable future for our business, our readers and our planet. This book is made from Forest Stewardship Council® certified paper.

Contents

Chapter One	1
Chapter Two	11
Chapter Three	15
Chapter Four	37
Chapter Five	67
Chapter Six	79
Chapter Seven	99
Chapter Eight	109
Chapter Nine	123
Chapter Ten	143
Chapter Eleven	171
Chapter Twelve	183

*Two things were certain every Saturday, growing up:
pancakes for breakfast and hiding behind a pillow with you at 7pm.
Thank you, Mum.*

One

The TARDIS: Time And Relative Dimension In Space, the most powerful spaceship in the known universe. A symbol of hope to all who encountered it. Dormant and presently uninhabited, its engines thrummed peacefully as if the Doctor's absence gave them their only real downtime. A gentle echo bounced off the white walls and rattled lightly around the TARDIS control room.

BANG!

The TARDIS doors swung open with great force, and Ruby and the Doctor burst through. They slammed the double doors shut behind them and both firmly pressed their backs against the cold wood for good measure.

Visibly shell-shocked, Ruby stood still for a moment, the only perceptible movement being the rise and fall of her chest as she attempted to regulate her laboured breathing. Overcome with exhaustion, she slowly slid to the floor. After a moment, the Doctor took a seat beside her. His expression matched hers, an almost identical cocktail of fear and concern. As he shifted his gaze slightly to find Ruby's eyes, his face immediately melted into his signature reassuring smile, which was promptly followed by the sound of raucous laughter.

Before she could fully process what might have been funny, Ruby found herself laughing too. The Doctor's energy was infectious, and she loved that about him. No matter the situation, whether it be giant lobsters hell-bent on world domination, alien cosplayers or sentient playgrounds manned by robot children, his smile was always a comfort to her.

From his pocket, he pulled out a small white cloth and a compact mirror and handed them both over to her. 'You, my dear, are gorgeous, ten out of ten, no notes. And you could probably pull off anything. That being said, the mud-sweat-soot combo doesn't really work for anybody. It's very… Dickens,' he joked, gesturing vaguely at her face with both index fingers.

'Oi!' She playfully punched him on the arm then opened up the compact. She found that she did indeed look like a Victorian street urchin, and it was not a good look. Her face was smudged with grime, and the mud in her hair made it look like she had opted for brown lowlights.

'Great man, Dickens—' The Doctor stopped abruptly, and his eyes widened as if he were reliving a traumatic memory. 'Grip was pure evil, though,' he shuddered.

'Aw, poor babes, did the nasty man hurt your little hand?' Ruby teased, as she finished wiping her face.

'First of all, rude,' he laughed. 'And second of all, Grip was the name of his pet raven and, as pet ravens go, he was a bit mean. Now Grip II, that was a majestic bird.

Excellent manners. Extremely intelligent. Great poker player too.'

'You played poker … with Charles Dickens's pet raven?' Ruby could hardly believe her ears but had experienced so much randomness and wonder on her travels with the Doctor that this particular story didn't seem all that implausible. 'I'll take your word for it.'

The Doctor grinned and nodded casually. 'Yeah, also did some ghostbusting with him …' He trailed off. He had caught a glimpse of something that made his smile disappear completely, along with his train of thought. The hem of his jet-black, straight-legged jumpsuit with chiffon overlay had been chewed. He gasped in horror. 'This was my favourite,' he cried, folding his arms with the defiant frustration of a toddler who had just been told 'no' for the first time.

Ruby smiled sympathetically at her friend and then happened to glance down at her own jeans. They had suffered the same fate. 'Mine too,' she moaned as she pulled her right foot to her face for closer inspection.

The Doctor shook his head, his frustration thawing into disappointment. 'Shame clothes can't regenerate.' He paused for a second. 'Or maybe they can? I guess anything is possible. Everything is possible!' He furrowed his brow, pursed his lips and concentrated really hard, willing regeneration energy into his tattered outfit …

Nothing.

'No, that's silly,' he concluded, slightly underwhelmed.

Ruby smiled, amused by his effortless whimsy and bespoke eccentricity. The Doctor often talked in a manner that made no sense to her, but this really had flown over her head. Having an alien as a new bestie had never been on the bingo card for her life, but she couldn't have been more thrilled. There was so much to learn, so much to experience; she had travelled through space and time and had found the universe outside her flat in London was infinite.

Before she could ask any clarifying questions, the Doctor sprang to his feet and skipped over to the TARDIS console. Then he swiftly whipped out his sonic screwdriver – a small, sleek flourish of silver and blue curves – and pointed it at the jukebox.

'"Baby Cakes, you just don't know!"' he sang with a smile before turning to his friend. 'I'd call that a win, wouldn't you?'

'Deffo,' Ruby replied. She mustered up all the strength her aching body could manage and clambered to her feet. She followed him to the console then leaned against the railings.

'It may have almost cost us our eyebrows, and some excellent outfits, but now the cyborg baby goats all have their original programming and are back to chewing curtains and jumping off sheet metal.'

They high-fived.

'And I can tick "milk a cyborg" off my bucket list,' Ruby said, shooting the Doctor a confident thumbs-up.

She watched as he danced effortlessly around the TARDIS console to the tune of the old-school garage music blasting from the jukebox, pushing and pressing buttons, flicking and twisting widgets in time to the music. He was truly a virtuoso conductor, and the console was his symphony orchestra.

Ruby's admiration of the Doctor was interrupted by a sudden thought. She struggled out of her chair and, like a child unable to conceptualise the meaning of personal space, she leant right into him and fiercely scrutinised his ageless skin. Not a single bead of sweat.

'How – are – you – not – knackered?' Every time she so much as exhaled her body ached. It reminded her of the one time she and her mates decided to take up running for a New Year's resolution. It hadn't lasted long because, after the first session, nobody could walk straight for about a week. Her mate Trudy had even ended up with tendonitis. She chuckled to herself, reliving the memory in her head. Although it hurt to laugh, this time the ache was warm and fuzzy.

She loved travelling with the Doctor but didn't half miss home sometimes.

The Doctor stepped back from her analytical gaze with a flourish. This was his current favourite topic of conversation. 'Time Lord biology, baby! It is truly marvellous.' He struck a pose, holding it just long enough to ensure Ruby had fully taken in how cool he looked. The image was only slightly undermined by the sight of his ankles poking involuntarily through his chewed hems. 'I don't know what the universe was doing when it designed humans, but it missed a few tricks there, I can tell you that much. I mean … only one heart? Could never be me. Well. Was once, kind of …'

Ruby turned slowly, mentally preparing for the long, painful waddle back to the comforting embrace of her chair.

'So! Where next?' the Doctor asked.

She halted mid-stride. 'Next? I've barely recovered from playing sheepdog all morning. Sheepdog? That can't be right, we were herding goats, not sheep. Goat dog? No, that's no better …'

'Come on! You're nineteen, a spring chicken!' The Doctor skipped around the console to meet his friend face to face. 'I have just the thing!'

He tore away from her and disappeared up the winding staircase and down the corridor. The TARDIS was massive and the Doctor was a hoarder so Ruby concluded that whatever this endeavour was could take anywhere between half a minute and several hours. She limped slowly over to her chair, reclined and took a deep breath in.

Before she could fully exhale, the Doctor had returned, cradling a shiny, metal dodecahedron in both hands.

'Ta-da!' he exclaimed enthusiastically. Like a magician, he waved his hand over the device in an attempt to add a sense of mystifying wonder to the experience.

'Brilliant...' Slightly disenchanted, Ruby inspected the instrument. To her it just looked like a plain shiny three-dimensional shape. 'What is it?'

'TA-DA!' the Doctor repeated with, somehow, even greater enthusiasm. Upon not receiving the desired reciprocal energy, he frowned. 'Tourist Artificial-Dimension Advocate.'

'Ah...' Ruby nodded slowly, feigning comprehension.

'You still haven't got a clue, have you?'

'Not a scooby,' she admitted confidently.

'T-A-D-A. Tourist Artificial-Dimension Advocate. TA-DA! It's essentially just a fancy travel agent. I won it in a badminton match against some Space Vikings. It is programmed to collate, suggest and project the best resorts in the known universe. In all universes!'

Ruby perked up, the adrenalin of excitement acting as a temporary cure to her ailing body. 'Are you saying what I think you're saying?' Nothing was ever as it seemed with the Doctor so she had found it was best practice to double-check from time to time.

He nodded enthusiastically. 'Yep, we're going on a proper holiday!'

'No running?'

'No running!' The Doctor took an index finger, crossed both his hearts and then turned to Ruby. 'I can't use it too often, because somebody gets jealous,' he whispered out of the corner of his mouth, discreetly pointing at the TARDIS console.

Fair enough, Ruby thought, sympathising with the TARDIS. The TA-DA seemed to be the equivalent of a self-service checkout, and she had always preferred human interaction.

'My last try for Ibiza had me solving riddles from a sentient honeycomb in Melissa Majoria.' The Doctor leant in closer. 'I'm convinced she misheard me on purpose.' He set the device to 'Random' and placed it on the floor. In an instant the top-facing pentagon retreated into itself and a bright burst of purple energy cascaded up and out of the TA-DA, filling the volume of the control room.

'Whoa...' Ruby whispered, transfixed by the amorphous blob of violet light that floated above her head. As she lifted an inquisitive finger to touch it, the energy snapped into a decisive shape. She watched as baths, fountains, busts and mosaics formed. The purple faded away and colours seeped in. Suddenly Ruby was standing in the middle of a Roman-looking spa that had manifested inside the TARDIS. She had visited Bath on a school trip once, but that couldn't compare.

'Is that meant to be there?' she laughed, pointing at the familiar console which had pushed through the perception filter to merge with a nearby fountain.

The Doctor tilted his head. 'She's very territorial,' he said. 'Rome, been there, done that.'

He promptly pulled out his sonic screwdriver and pointed it at the TA-DA. In the blink of an eye the spa disappeared, and Ruby was standing on a beach with onyx-black sand beneath her feet. She could feel it between her toes, even though she was wearing shoes. Warm and grainy.

Before she could look up to take in the rest of her surroundings, the beach had disappeared, replaced with crimson mud and four suns in the sky. That vision too faded as a conveyor belt of luxury destinations sped past her face. It all went so fast she could hardly keep up. She had done VR before, but this was a whole new world… literally. Several new worlds! Glimpses of pools, mountains and palm trees flashed past her eyes. It was exhilarating. Moments later, she felt a gentle nudge in her side.

'Go on,' said the Doctor. 'Yell stop.'

She took a deep breath then yelled at the top of her lungs. 'STOOOOP!' The carousel halted abruptly, and the TARDIS jolted. It began to shake violently, knocking the TA-DA over. At its collapse, the violet energy returned to its former amorphous shape and was immediately sucked back into the device.

'Oops.' The Doctor ran over to the console. 'Must've accidentally set the link between the TARDIS and the TA-DA to autopilot.' The Doctor stabilised the shaking and smiled. 'Well, I guess now we're on our way.'

'But to where?' Ruby asked. She could still feel the aftershocks of the turbulence in her legs and so held on to the railing for good measure.

'Chimandra Galaxy, Yewa, the Gardens of Kubuntu – Resting Place of the Eternals. Says here, the most peaceful place in the universe,' the Doctor said, reading the screen on the console carefully. 'We haven't landed yet but...'

Without hesitation, Ruby ran to the doors and opened them up. She knew the oxygen and mavity bubbles around the TARDIS would keep her safe, so she stepped out and found herself floating in space between two identical icy blue planets.

She looked down at her feet. She was standing on a cloud of burnt orange and crimson crystal. It acted as a sort of bridge between the two planets. 'Wow...' she sighed. A word popped into her head. 'Sublime.' She didn't know why but that was it. It was sublime, it went beyond mere beauty. The overwhelming sense of vastness and magnitude left an impression on her soul.

The Doctor poked his head out. 'Come on, get packing, I've made a booking!'

Two

A short while later Ruby stood at the TARDIS doors, brimming with the eager anticipation of a child on their way to Chessington for the first time. At her feet were four small suitcases, lined up as if they were queuing to exit with her.

What waits beyond those doors? she thought to herself. *Endless wonder!*

She tapped her foot rhythmically, her patience wearing thin. She looked at an imaginary watch on her wrist.

Then she let out a long, exasperated sigh and threw her head back. 'Doooctoooor!' she moaned.

Before she could manifest the rest of her complaint, the Doctor appeared, sporting a summery printed boiler suit and holding a matching clutch. He struck a pose, brandishing his bag as if it were a Spanish flamenco fan.

'Absolute slay!' Ruby applauded in full support of this display of elegance, grace and flare.

As the Doctor strutted towards her, she took in the burnt red, muted pink and deep blue hues of his garments. His clothes testified to the spectrum of his personality. He was so bright and vivid, he burst with colour and depth from the inside out.

The Doctor smiled. 'Now this, I looove this.' He stopped, affronted by Ruby's assortment of luggage. He looked at her then back down at her queue of suitcases. 'You moving out?'

'Is that all you're taking?' Ruby replied, nodding at the clutch, shocked that someone with the Doctor's pedigree of taste would have packed so little.

'I'll have you know I've got three weeks' worth of stunners in here!'

Everything with the Doctor was bigger on the inside, Ruby remembered: his ship, his bags, his pockets. 'Well, we haven't all got transdimensional thingies.'

'I'm sure I have a dimensionally transcendental bum bag around here somewhere.' He made sure to emphasise the words 'dimensionally' and 'transcendental', as a form of light education.

Ruby smiled at the thought of herself wearing a bum bag on holiday, reimagining herself as a Hawaiian-shirted dad who had dragged his reluctant family to the beach for a bonding sesh. She laughed to herself, envisioning the full get-up: sandals, cargos and a visor. 'I'll take my chances with the suitcases. One for each season, just in case.' She tilted her head inquisitively. 'Did you ever get readings on the climate?'

The Doctor stepped over the suitcases and moved towards the doors. 'Nah, the readings were all over the place. Very strange. Good news is that the atmosphere's breathable, so let's leave all that here and scope out the scenery.' As he put his hand on the door lock, an idea formed in his head. Ruby could tell, she always knew when he had an idea because his eyes brightened. 'Or better yet, we go source some local garms!'

'Local garms, I love it.' Ruby's excitement quickly shifted to concern. 'Is it not like cultural appropriation, though?'

The Doctor placed a hand on her shoulder. 'When in Rome, do as the Romans do. Now, if you were to take the clothes back to London and flog them on Portobello Road, that would be bad vibes ...' He looked up, a new thought. 'Alternatively, this lot could be a culture of nudists and our worries are irrelevant. Anyway, apparently they have every single spa treatment ever. And babe, I'm telling you, you haven't lived until you've had a Venusian deep-tissue massage.'

The two friends stood frozen for a moment. The energy of the endless possibility of a new experience built in their toes and rushed through their legs then upwards until their bodies could contain it no longer. They grabbed each other's hands and shared a little jig of excitement, prancing around in circles, giggling wildly.

Eventually they collected themselves and regained their composure. The Doctor smiled and then reached his hand out towards the lock.

He paused, a small expectant hesitation, before he opened the door.

Three

The TARDIS had landed in an empty cul-de-sac off the main street. Ruby could see the market at the junction. Surrounding the circular road were identical, neatly kept houses, each with a meticulously maintained front garden.

'Hmm...' the Doctor mused as his eyes passed over the houses surrounding him. 'Why have a plant pot without any plants?'

Ruby looked around. Sure enough, every shiny plant pot and immaculate flowerbed was empty.

'Weird,' she said.

'I hope this isn't another duck pond situ,' murmured the Doctor. 'That wouldn't be cute.'

'Duck pond?'

'Ignore me.' He smiled.

Ruby's eyes had taken a few moments to adjust to the Yewan sun's cold white light. The sky was a vast expanse of lavender, stretching endlessly to the horizon. No clouds, just several swirling purple hues. It reminded her of a marble cake. Cutting through the atmosphere above her was the celestial bridge she'd stood on earlier, an ethereal band of shimmering light, arcing gracefully across the heavens, connecting Yewa with its sister planet. It was as beautiful to look up at as it had been to look down on. And in the distance, Bia, its massive form occupying as much space as the sun itself, casting a diffused, slightly golden glow over the cul-de-sac.

Ruby's gaze lingered. She took an intentional breath in, allowing the feeling – a mix of awe and wonder – to wash over her. She turned to the Doctor, who was now in one of the gardens, his expression distant and contemplative.

'What is it?' she asked, her voice breaking the silence.

The Doctor looked down at the ground and performed a couple of small inquisitive jumps. He inhaled deeply, taking in a long, deliberate sniff. 'There's something… puzzling. Beneath my feet. Can you feel it? That energy… a low-level telepathic field.' He jumped again. 'Icy but not cold, firm yet not unyielding, plus the telepathy. It's probably not ice at all.'

He lay down flat on his belly to inspect the ground. 'Yup, not ice – crystals,' he said as Ruby joined him. 'See, light is made up of electromagnetic waves of various wavelengths. When light hits an object, some wavelengths are absorbed, and others are reflected. Now, the reflected wavelengths are what we perceive as colour. White light is a combination of all visible wavelengths of light. It includes all the colours of the spectrum: red, orange, yellow, green, blue, indigo and violet.'

Ruby looked closely. She could see them all and it shifted her perspective slightly: for something so plain and basic as the colour white to be made up of all the other colours in the spectrum was somehow beautiful.

The Doctor shot to his feet. 'There's something else beneath the surface. I suspect tunnels,' he jumped again, 'ooh, or catacombs... very nice.' He sniffed the air repeatedly. 'This place is *sniff* old, *sniff* ancient, even. Deffo catacombs.'

As Ruby got to her feet, a young man appeared out of nowhere, tearing past them and knocking her off balance, before disappearing into one of the nearby houses. As Ruby tried to find her footing, she slipped on the ice. It was one of those falls where your whole life flashes before your eyes in the seconds it takes for mavity to do its bidding. Luckily, before she could find out what glacial, alien earth tasted like, the Doctor caught her.

'Careful!' he yelled at no one in particular. 'Watch where you're going!' He pulled his friend to her feet and dusted her off. 'Are you okay?'

'Yeah, I'm fine.'

'He didn't even stop!' The Doctor turned and yelled in the man's direction: 'Rude!' But he was long gone.

'I'm all right Doctor, let's leave it.' Ruby took him by the hand and dragged him towards the main street. 'Come on, that TA-DA says there's a personal massage table waiting for me.'

She watched as the Doctor made a deliberate effort not to let his frustration ruin her holiday. He shook it off.

Arm in arm, they stepped into the street where the

main market resided. Ruby looked around in amazement, her senses immediately lavished by a kaleidoscope of soothing sounds and delightful scents.

As they walked, they passed textiles in rich, warm tones fluttering softly in the mild breeze, creating a moving mosaic of patterns and textures. Laughter and light-hearted chatter filled the air, mingling with the rhythmic clinking of glass jars.

They passed stall after stall, fully stocked with lush fruits and vegetables. All of it was irregular in shape, nothing round or flawless, which made them strangely perfect. The intense, sweet, tangy scent of fresh citrus fruits mingled with subtle hints of freshly baked bread and exotic spices wafting through the air, inviting and warm.

A tear had formed in Ruby's eye. She let it fall down her cheek and then wiped it away. She wasn't sure why she was crying; she wasn't sad and had been to alien planets before. But this planet felt different, like it was communicating with her directly. It vibrated her soul gently. She looked to the Doctor to find a tear had formed in his eye too.

'Most peaceful place in the universe… they weren't lying,' Ruby said, dabbing her face dry.

'Come on, Ruby,' the Doctor said softly. 'Kubuntu is this way.'

'How do you know that?'

'The Gardens of Kubuntu are one of the 700 ancient

wonders of the universe. They are located at the centremost point of the southern pole of Yewa's axis, which is –' he stuck his finger in his mouth and then pointed it to the sky – 'that way! Left! It's one of my party tricks: give me any planet and I can find the equator, north and south pole. My internal compass is on point!' He beamed with pride.

They came to a fork in the street and turned left, finding themselves in the midst of a local festival. The energy was a little different around this corner. The initial tranquillity Ruby had experienced was still at its heart, but now it was surrounded by a buzz of excitement. The air was filled with a symphony: the melodic hum of hovering transportation, the rhythmic beats of percussive instruments, and something else, something less tangible but not completely intangible. What was it? Goodwill, good energy, positivity.

The market burst with lively colour and elaborate costumes, which aggressively contrasted with the cool, glacial nature of their surroundings. In the distance, at the outskirts of the market, a crowd had formed.

'Wonder what that's all about,' she asked, pointing towards the gathering.

'Let's have a gander! Check-in won't be for another couple of hours anyway.'

As they skipped towards the crowd in the clearing, Ruby took in the vibrant mosaic of food trucks and multi-tiered hover stalls that lined the street. They were crafted from metals that shifted and shimmered as white sunlight bounced off the icy peaks. As Ruby let it all sink in, she found herself noticing everything. All her senses had heightened since leaving the TARDIS.

Her first observation: the people of Yewa were unusually tall; even the toddlers seemed large for their age. She observed their skin; they were tanned like unbaked terracotta clay. Each person, even the children, had shimmering, bioluminescent tattoos that decorated their whole bodies. She found herself staring again; she'd always been taught it was rude, but she couldn't help herself. Each Yewan was so unique and individual yet familiar in appearance. Pockets of life on Yewa popped in front of them as they journeyed through the market towards the crowd in the clearing. People engaged in animated conversations and gossip; merchants noisily negotiated trades with patrons; children ran through the streets with toy windmills and kites.

'People on Earth don't fly kites any more, do they? It's a shame.' The Doctor shook his head in mourning for the lost art form.

'Or maybe they never did, and *Mary Poppins* was just a very effective illusion shown too often in the school holidays,' Ruby replied. 'You know, that thing where you see something once and then you can't stop seeing it. Maybe people never really flew kites back in the day; we just think they did because of the film.'

'Aah, so the increase in perceived frequency is not due to an actual increase in the occurrence of the word or concept, but rather due to your heightened awareness and selective attention... interesting. You might be on to something there. After this, we'll take a trip to London 1910 and see what's up.' The Doctor nodded, thoroughly impressed with Ruby's level of critical thinking.

'Don't think I'll ever get over this,' Ruby sighed. 'It reminds me of home. Is that weird? A billion miles away, and I'm feeling at home.'

'Think of it this way. There are infinite connections between the universe and humans. Everything in the universe came from the supernova of a star billions of years ago. The end of a star's life looks a lot like the birth of a human cell. The complex web of neurones inside your brain is reflected in the cosmic network of galaxies that make up that very universe. Inside that wonderful human brain of yours, there is an incomprehensible level of complexity and self-organisation that mirrors the inner mechanics of the universe itself. Now if I designed the universe and I had created something so impossibly perfect, I'd make sure that all life got a taste.'

Ruby teared up again and, as she sniffed, she scented aromas wafting through the air, an intoxicating blend of fragrances that tickled her nostrils. Her belly grumbled audibly.

The Doctor grinned. 'Hungry?' Ruby nodded enthusiastically. 'Me too!'

They stopped by the first food truck they saw. A jolly Yewan man appeared at the truck's window. His large frame took up most of the opening. 'Hellooo, I am Tamotah. You are blessed and highly favoured by the Gardens of Kubuntu and crowned in the light of our ancestors' sun.' He smiled and his tattoos gleamed.

'Hello, I'm the Doctor and this is Ruby.'

Tamotah's smile faded slightly, as did his tattoos, but the Doctor continued, self-assured.

'You are blessed and highly favoured by the Gardens of Kubuntu and crowned in the light of your ancestors' sun,' he said.

Tamotah brightened once again. 'No charge,' he said as he handed them two skewers of spiced dried fruit. 'You must be here for the resort. I appreciate your taking the time to respect our customs. But be careful. Not everyone around here is a fan of aliens.' Tamotah held up a hand. 'Enjoy the festival! First Kaloa in 200 years.'

'How long?' the Doctor began. Then he paused, seemingly unable to press further with his line of questioning.

Ruby sensed it immediately: he had been interrupted by the same sensation she was experiencing. It was a growing dread so powerful it made her feel queasy.

Tamotah frowned and spoke urgently. 'The Yewa believe there are higher senses above most of the universe's basic five. Instinct is the most powerful one. Get off the street, something wicked is coming.'

As if on cue, the sound of a skirmish rattled behind them. The Doctor turned round to see a cluster of three men standing over a young Yewan man.

The gang didn't resemble the other Yewans. They were shorter and slender, with the same orange skin tone but somewhat paler and lacking the signature tattoos. They moved with forceful coordination and synchronicity, jostling and shoving the Yewan man to the ground.

A Yewan mother broke away from her children, who had previously been playing with a small pet polar bear. She grabbed one of the men by the shoulder and forced him away.

From under his clothes, the man revealed a weapon and shot two white laser blasts near her feet. 'Keep back,' he said, 'or your children will stand witness to their mother's death.'

A wave of terror washed over the locals. Some cowered, rooted to the spot in fear, whilst others fled. One of the attackers overturned the market stall of the Yewan mother as further deterrent. He sized her up, but she was unmoved. She stood tall and brave. So he spat at her and then returned his attention to the man on the ground.

The aggressors' collective energy was palpable. Ruby could almost feel their hatred in her own limbs, paralysing her. But the Doctor handed his skewer to Ruby and marched forward.

'Hey! Hey!' he yelled. 'Leave them alone!' He pushed and squeezed through frenzied market-goers, some attempting to escape the violence and some hell-bent on ignoring the trouble altogether.

Ruby forced her legs to work and followed the Doctor, anxious to not be separated from her friend. By the time she arrived, the attackers had dispersed, and she could see no sign of them. The Doctor was helping the Yewan man pick himself up from the floor. 'Are you okay?'

'Yes, I'm fine,' the man replied. He looked it, not a single bruise or cut on him.

'I'm the Doctor, this is Ruby.'

'You are blessed and highly favoured by the Gardens of Kubuntu and crowned in the light of your ancestors' sun,' Ruby said with a smile.

'I'm Mo.' The young man shuffled awkwardly and then bowed his head to avoid eye contact. 'I'm sorry.'

'What for?' the Doctor asked, puzzled.

Mo turned to Ruby. 'I made you fall. I was trying to get away from them. It's not like me to be so rude. They just wouldn't leave me alone.'

'Ah.' Ruby realised Mo was the man who'd almost floored her earlier. 'I forgive you,' she said, and smiled to see him stifle a grin. 'Why were they attacking you?'

Mo yawned. 'It's just the way the Bia are.'

'The Bia?'

'Neighbours from their sister planet,' the Doctor informed her.

Ruby nodded. 'Ah, the ones across the space bridge. Gotcha!' She flashed him a thumbs-up. Mo tilted his head, as if unsure what this gesture meant.

'What about the police?' Ruby continued. 'These Bia can't go around shooting off their mouths and laser guns without—'

'Best to just leave it. I have to go, I'm late. There are people waiting for me.' Mo raised both his hands to Ruby and the Doctor.

Once they mirrored him, he pressed his palms up against theirs and wrapped his thumb around the back of their hands.

'Cute, it's like a hand hug! Adorable, that,' the Doctor said. 'Are you sure we can't help you with—'

'No that's fine,' Mo said and then ran off, disappearing into the mass of Yewan bodies.

The Doctor had that look on his face again.

'What?' Ruby asked.

'He was a bit... all over the place. You know, you meet people and you try not to judge or put them in boxes but...' The Doctor made an attempt to choose his words carefully. 'He didn't quite fit. Blunt, awkward, grinning, apologising. Character is consistent and Mo is... well...'

The Doctor looked around; everyone had returned to business as usual. Like nothing had happened. 'And another thing, where did they go?'

'Who?' said Ruby.

'The Bia, where did they go?' The Doctor frowned. 'There are clear sight lines from this spot, and they just poofed into thin air.'

'Must have just disappeared into the crowds?'

Deep in thought, the Doctor sniffed the air. He caught a metallic, burning scent, faint but unmistakeable, and nodded. Thermal teleportation? Maybe that was why it was so warm on this icy-looking planet with a cold white sun: the conversion of thermal energy to power teleports. That would explain how people here could move so fast.

Still. He had promised Ruby no running, and he was not in the business of breaking promises. He felt the sense of peace settling about them, soft as snow, but suddenly he didn't trust it. It was as if the place was urging him not to ask questions.

But I have questions, the Doctor thought.

He could see the pieces of a puzzle forming, but didn't have enough to put them together. He could feel his grasp of time slipping slightly too. Eventually his spiral of consciousness was interrupted by a sweet aroma. He snapped back into reality and there was Ruby, smiling, holding his skewer under his nose and her own to her lips.

The Doctor took the snack from his friend and was again welcomed by the smell of spices from a distant galaxy. He and Ruby locked eyes and each took a bite of their fruit.

'Mmmm!' The Doctor revelled in the burst of flavour. 'Gorgeous!'

Ruby nodded, practically inhaling the rest of the skewer.

The Doctor took her stick and dropped it with his in a litter basket as he set off again with Ruby at his side. But they had only managed a few steps before they both stopped simultaneously.

'Doctor...'

'Ruby...'

Abruptly, they burst out laughing; it was the type of laughter that was never-ending, uncontrollable, involuntary and hurt in the best way possible. It came from the depths of their bellies.

The Doctor could literally feel the increased levels of dopamine shooting around his brainstems. He saw Ruby's eyes had dilated. Both of his hearts were beating so hard he thought they might give in. The left one had caught up to the right and then overtaken it. He felt lopsided.

'That is serious fruit,' Ruby declared. 'I feel like I could literally wrestle a bear and win.'

'Mount Everest? Twenty-minute jog, max,' the Doctor joked. 'Still, we are on holiday, so maybe we should take it a bit easier...'

The side-effects of their snack attack soon wore off, and the two of them set off again, their normal selves. Well, almost.

'That stuff's legend,' said Ruby. 'I don't ache half as much as I did.'

'Got some pep in your step?' The Doctor nodded approvingly. 'Yeah. Me too.'

They embedded themselves within an audience gathered in the courtyard, where the music was intoxicating, explaining why no one seemed shaken or affected by the earlier commotion – it was all-encompassing. Interlocking rhythmic patterns, with drums and other percussion, layered to create a driving beat. A repetitive groove formed the foundation for a trance-like melody of brass and wind instruments, playing a catchy call-and-response.

Across the space, on a raised platform, behind a deep pink tulle veil, an obscured silhouette swayed to the rhythms. In the centre, a group of masquerade dancers were performing. Although they moved with perfect uniformity, each dancer's attire differed. They wore elaborate costumes and masks made out of carved crystal. The facial features of the masks were exaggerated and expressive with enlarged eyes, open mouths and the signature bioluminescent tattoos.

As the dancers shook to the sound of the drums, the sea of vibrant colours, intricate patterns and symbolic designs that made up their costumes blurred Ruby's vision. There were so many fabrics, beads, shells and feathers, her eyes could barely keep up. Although the characters' faces were inanimate, Ruby felt like she could sense the spiritual qualities of each one's mask, like they were communicating to her who they were and how they felt.

The Doctor felt a tap on his shoulder and turned to find a jolly woman next to him grinning, revealing a row of gold grilles, each tooth set with tiny, sparkling gems that caught the light. 'The design of each mask carries a symbolic message from the Yewan ancestral spirits. That one there is Kubuntu, the first ancestor,' she said. 'Are you foreigners? You look like foreigners,' she continued with a smile.

The Doctor noticed Ruby shift slightly and put a reassuring hand on her arm. 'It's not a bad word everywhere.'

Ruby nodded, seemingly more at ease.

'Ooh, now that is a look,' he exclaimed.

Ruby followed the Doctor's finger to a veiled androgynous dancer. Their fingertips and toes were dyed deep mustard yellow, and they were adorned from head to toe in jewellery. Silver anklets, rings and chains tinkled as they danced. Around their neck was a necklace featuring five gemstones: two diamonds, two amethysts, and in the centre, the most perfect moonstone.

The jolly woman waved goodbye to them and stepped into the centre to chronicle the message and meaning of the dance. She was an elderly woman with a regal bearing, her silver hair neatly braided and adorned with tiny beads that glimmered in the light. She wore a flowing robe of deep indigo, embroidered with intricate gold patterns that shimmered as she moved. Her voice, deep, rich and melodic, commanded the attention of the captive audience as she regaled them with the tale, and the dancers retold the story of Yewa and Bia through their graceful motions.

> 'At the beginning of time, when the universe was both vast and nothing, Chimandra was born.
>
> A tiny galaxy on the edge of the universe, Chimandra in turn birthed Kubuntu, and Kubuntu was the first life and the moon was her soul. For millennia Kubuntu existed in peaceful solitude and her heart grew full of creativity and her mind overflowed with unimaginable imagination. Kubuntu toyed with many forms of life but none found favour and they all ebbed away in an Empire of the Lost and Damned.
>
> One day, Kubuntu plucked a Crystal from her own being and shaped two planets in her image. And so Yewa and Bia were born out of the fabric of her existence. Kubuntu gifted Bia wealth, strength and industry, then descended to gift Yewa balance, beauty and gentleness.
>
> As the planets flourished and her descendants multiplied, Kubuntu grew old and so she retired to Yewa and planted her Garden, the resting place for all beauty and in turn her final resting place. She had given life and existed well for many years, but all things must end.

> With her final breath, she connected our two planets, using her spirit as a celestial bridge, linking their prosperity for all eternity. Kubuntu's final wish was that every year, the heir of Yewa and the heir of Bia renew their spiritual link at the Ijoa, in the Garden of Kubuntu, to remind us that our connection and harmony with one another are the adhesive that binds our cosmos.
>
> There was a time when, once each year, the Kaloa Festival celebrated our union and honoured Kubuntu's act of sacrifice, plucking the Crystal from her being to give life to us all. But for so long the Crystal has been lost and the Kaloa have stopped, though none may say why. Still, today our joy is reborn. This will be our first Kaloa in countless years and we give thanks to the ancestors for reconnecting this generation to our elders.'

'No one knows why they stopped?' The Doctor felt unsatisfied with this notion. No one knew, and it sounded like they were all content with that. 'So an intrinsic part of their culture hasn't happened in 200 years, that's 200 times. I'd be asking questions after the third, wouldn't you?'

'Maybe the important thing to focus on is that it's happening now,' said Ruby. 'A new beginning.'

It was an excellent point, yet something was niggling at the Doctor. Instinct. His feelings were all over the place. He felt peace but had questions; everything felt contradictory.

'Cirque du Soleil have nothing on these lot,' Ruby said, in awe of the dancers as they performed mavity-defying feats of acrobatics. Flips and twists galore in an emphatic display of agility and strength. The people of Yewa danced too. The choreography was energetic and dynamic: quick footwork, jumps and spins.

Despite the energy, the composition of the masquerade dance was fluid and graceful. All present moved in smooth unison, and the Doctor and Ruby found themselves moving with the locals in perfect synchronicity.

I don't remember learning this in PE, Ruby thought.

A performer stepped out and addressed the people. 'Remember our dance is an offering to our ancestors, our dance is an offering to Kubuntu. Dance in gratitude, dance with vitality, dance in celebration of your life force,' he said before returning to the dance himself. They moved as if their lives depended on it. As the drums crescendoed and the dancing intensified, a wave of fresh emotion washed over the Doctor.

He felt liberated. Carefree. Burdenless.

In due course, the music stopped and the dance ended.

'How did we pick that up?' Ruby gasped, out of breath. 'It's not like I'm wearing those psychic earrings so...'

'I dunno!' The Doctor shrugged with a smile. 'That was amazing!' It was unlike him to not have a super-in-depth, complex answer laced with scientific jargon that she could barely understand, but Ruby figured that he had found himself deep in the holiday spirit and decided not to jinx it with further questioning.

The performers turned to the audience and bowed. They then turned towards the pink tulle veil. The silhouette stood and pulled back the curtains. She was captivating, a mesmerising blend of ethereal elegance and diaphanous charm. The pearlescent tattoos on her flawless skin shimmered softly under the cool light of the Yewan sun. Her eyes reflected the hues of the celestial sky, a mix of amethyst and azure which echoed the very nature of her home planet. Her elongated limbs and fluidity of movement were almost hypnotic. She smiled and applauded regally. The dancer who had played Kubuntu lowered their veil to address the woman on the plinth.

'Nazari, heir of Kubuntu, our original ancestor, will you dance for your people?'

The crowd erupted in encouraging cheers. Nazari smiled. She slowly got to her feet and made her way from the throne down to the ground, fuelled by the ovation from her people. As she descended, the rhythm of the drums blended with the rampant applause in such a way that Ruby could feel it in her chest, and her heart welcomed it. As soon as Nazari's foot touched the floor, the drumming ceased. The crowd listened intently with silent anticipation. You could hear a pin drop.

Nazari bowed humbly. 'I dance to serve my people,' she said with a smile. 'I dance to—'

Suddenly the sound of drums started up again. Nazari looked to the instrumentalists, confused. So did Ruby.

The musicians weren't playing. So where was the thump of percussion coming from?

The Doctor looked around for the source of the drumming. It was coming from beneath their feet.

The floor began to shake violently; objects fell off stalls and hit the crystal ground. People struggled to remain upright. They held on to anything they could: stalls, lampposts and even each other.

'An earthquake?' Ruby asked.

The Doctor turned to her and grabbed her hand, scanning the ground beneath him with his sonic screwdriver. He huffed. 'That's not possible, earthquakes are caused by the friction between the edges of tectonic plates. When the stress on the edge of a plate is overcome with friction, that releases energy in waves that travel through the planet's surface, which causes the shaking we feel.'

'So…?'

'So… according to the sonic, Yewa exists on one massive tectonic plate. There are no plate boundaries.'

'So what's causing the shaking?'

The sound and shake of three more underground explosions came in quick succession. The force of the detonations threw the masquerade dancers off their feet, propelled them into the crowd. It was pandemonium as people once again scattered in attempts to find safety.

Once the Doctor's initial shock and disorientation cleared, he found his bearings in the thick veil of smoke rising from the ground. The Doctor checked on Ruby, who nodded that she was fine, and then scanned the crowd with the sonic too.

The panic grew worse as a new sound cut through the hubbub. The sharp zing of weapons firing. The sound of danger and death.

Without a second's pause, the Doctor ran towards it through the smoke.

He found three masked individuals on powered snowboards, circling Nazari, firing their weapons at the ground near her feet. *Intimidation?* he wondered. *Or are they just rubbish shots?*

Dancing and weaving, Nazari dodged the oppressive fire as best she could but was soon backed against the plinth she had descended from.

Before the masked figures could press home their attack, the Doctor once again aimed his sonic. He scrambled the snowboards' power source, and the men were sent crashing to the ground. Before they could mount any further attack, the Yewan masquerade performers aligned themselves like rugby players ready for a lineout, and launched a dancer into the air. The dancer collided with the man nearest to Nazari, knocking him to the ground just as he'd got back to his feet, wrestling the weapon from his hand. The performer playing Kubuntu clawed at another of the attackers, forcibly removing his mask. It was one of the three Bia men from earlier, the ones who'd attacked Mo.

The Doctor looked around to see if he could find Nazari. The way the Bia had encircled her, she had clearly been the target of the attack; he had to make sure she was safe. But she was nowhere to be found.

Had she slipped away in all the chaos or had more Bia taken her hostage?

He shifted his attention back to where the masquerade dancers had been fighting the Bia, but now they stood alone in the clearing, the foes vanished. The Doctor moved towards the performers, but as he did, they flinched and fled into the market. He looked around the clearing to find all the spectators and instrumentalists had dispersed too. Ruby, standing alone now, shrugged at him. The once busy market, which had bustled with vivacious life and pure joy, had become a ghost town.

'Come on,' said the Doctor, 'let's get you to the resort.' His mind was made up; he had to get Ruby to safety and then come back to figure out what was going on. Right now, it just didn't make any sense.

He smiled. That was the best part.

Four

The Doctor had only been on Yewa for an hour, but he had a million questions. Why were the Bia so angry? 'It's just the way they are' was a cop-out; they must want something. What did they want? To intimidate but not murder? But why? To what end? Mo? There was something about him; he didn't quite fit. No, that wasn't fair, bad Doctor. He knew better than to judge. He and Ruby continued their walk, once again arm in arm.

'Ooh, that fruit stick is wearing off big time,' Ruby groaned. The Doctor could sense the weariness returning to her body as he found himself providing extra support as they journeyed out of the market. 'The only thing keeping me upright is the thought of being wrapped up in that crisp white hotel bedding ... and you, of course!'

The Doctor bowed his head slightly, grateful for the acknowledgement.

They finally arrived at a plain at the edge of the city centre. Across the level surface of flawless crystal, in the near distance, stood a crystalline terraced garden complex, towering over them. The garden's terraces were adorned with vibrant, luminescent flora that glowed softly, casting a soothing light. Water cascaded gently down the crystal steps, and the sound of light rain filled the air. The sun had taken on a golden hue, which refracted through the water and bounced off the crystalline surface, creating a dazzling display of ever-shifting colour.

'Oh wow ...' they said with simultaneous awe.

The Doctor looked up in enchantment. 'Welcome to the Gardens of Kubuntu Resort and Spa.' He was relieved to see a variety of multicoloured hanging trees, plants and shrubs spilling out over the sides in abundance.

Well, that's good to know, he thought to himself. One less thing to worry about: there were plants on Yewa. He hadn't seen a single one thus far; he would have been dumbfounded if he had arrived at a Garden and there wasn't so much as a leaf to be seen.

The resort had been constructed using a series of ascending terraces, like enormous multi-levelled steps, and each tier hosted a bountiful garden. It reminded him of the Aztec pyramids; however, these were eye-catchingly arranged upside down.

Ruby pointed to the bottom tier, which was the smallest of all. 'How is that balancing?' she asked.

'Inverse quantum physics.' The Doctor took a breath in preparation for a long explanation, then grinned. 'Sorry, you're officially on holiday. No complicated science lessons for you, please and thank you.'

As they got closer to the Gardens, the finer details became clearer. The Doctor marvelled at their irrigation system – a complex network of canals and pumps that brought water from the crystal blue Ratehs river which flowed alongside the Garden's gates.

The gates! The Doctor had been so wrapped up in the inner mechanics of the sprinkler system he hadn't realised what was happening at the gates. Something had shifted, something in the air had changed. There was a small energetic crowd at the gates. But the hustle and bustle wasn't the same, it wasn't goodwill or positive energy, not at all. It was a demonstration. A small group of fifteen or so Yewans, shouting and jeering at a woman who stood between them and the Gardens. They were led by another woman.

'We demand access to the Gardens. You cannot deny us! We are the Firebrand, and we will be heard.'

Ruby made her way to the front of the angry mob, eager to see what all the fuss was about. She hadn't been on Yewa very long but for somewhere that had boasted it was 'the most relaxing place in the known universe', it really hadn't been living up to the hype.

As she squeezed through the jungle of angry fists, she could feel the shared grievance amongst the protestors. The ignited passion and conviction within them rumbled in her bones. It made her feel fuzzy, but not in a pleasant way, more like the edges of her very being had been blended with those of these vexed strangers. She was dizzy with anger, but fought to remain vertical.

The woman leading the mob was smaller than the average Yewan, and her skin was covered densely in tattoos. She was more tattoo than anything else. As her voice boomed, it silenced the raging crowd, and they hung on her every word. Ruby noted that most of those present, including the woman, had been in the audience at the festival at the time of the attacks.

The Doctor stepped past her to address the mob. 'Hey, hey, hey, what's going on?' he asked the leader with a friendly smile and in a tone he must have specifically engineered for de-escalating intense situations.

The woman turned to him, looked him up and down and turned her attention back to her protestors. The Doctor's mouth dropped open in disbelief, and Ruby couldn't blame him. Usually people told him everything; he had one of those faces. Evil masterminds couldn't help themselves: they just blurted out their entire plans, sometimes without him even really asking.

'For too long, the Yewan people have suffered in silence whilst "high-borns" luxuriate at their expense,' said the woman. 'And now the Gardens are sanctuary for those who attack Yewan people on Yewan land! I say no more! We will live in the new era of violent liberation!'

The Doctor's ears pricked. 'Violent liberation, got it. Great stuff! How about we —'

Another amazonian woman stepped forward, all that stood between the protestors and the resort Gardens. 'Fala,' she said in a gentle voice, 'if you do not leave, you know what will happen and you know it cannot be stopped once activated.'

Fala turned from her followers swiftly in order to face her. 'And you! Don't get me started on you, Mya. You work for them. We know the Bia are here, and that more are coming for the Ijoa. Bring the fugitives out to face justice or we will enter and gain vengeance for ourselves. We breathe recycled air and cannot offer sacrifice to the ancestors in the inner sanctum. We cannot heal the sick, but that is fine with you because at least rich men can sauna and bathe in our milk and honey.'

Mya shook her head, apparently disappointed. 'Fala, please, I have to warn you—'

'Mya, I have to warn you.' Fala rolled her shoulders back, puffed out her chest and stepped forward. At this motion the rest of the Firebrand stood to attention. Although they looked like a ragtag bunch, for the most part they moved with precision and direction.

Mya stepped forward and met Fala's eyes. As she stared into them, her steely expression of resistance shifted, and a look of pity melted through. She put her hand to Fala's cheek, cradling her face gently. 'You have changed. What happened to you?'

Unmoved, Fala knocked Mya's hand away from her face. 'I am the child of my environment. Bring out the heathens or we will take them by force.'

'I will not repeat myself, Fala. The Bia you seek are not here.'

'Could I just interject…?' Again, before the Doctor could finish his sentence, Fala had retreated and returned to her followers. Then the drumming began. Rhythmic, pulsating, urgent.

Ruby could feel a shift in energy as the Firebrand's chants accompanied the drums. The rhythm continued to build, fuelled by frustration, anger and hope. Sustained by solidarity. There was a sense of urgency and determination, an electric atmosphere pulsating. Ruby sat down, her head rushing with waves of emotion. Emotions that were both hers but simultaneously not hers. This place was seriously messing with her head.

The Doctor rushed to her side, a look of concern on his face. 'You all right? he asked.

Ruby looked up at him as he put his hand on her shoulder. 'Whoa!'

'What?'

'It's just… are you okay? It's like – well, it's weird.'

She didn't know how she knew or even how to tell him, but she could taste his guilt. It was oaky and mature and bitter. She smacked her tongue against the roof of her mouth, trying to shift the flavour of ancient guilt. She looked into his eyes and felt a sting behind her own. This guilt long outdated her and she could feel how heavily it weighed on him. *Better not*, she thought before gently pulling away.

As she broke contact, she felt a lot lighter, no longer sharing his feelings. 'Never mind me,' she said. 'Sort this!'

The Doctor took a moment to take stock of his surroundings. Ever since he had landed on Yewa, he had felt a little on the back foot – one step behind – and the truth was, he enjoyed it. This was why he travelled, to be surprised, caught off guard. He loved the complexity of everything. It made him feel warm, like a hot soup on a cold day. He ground his feet into his shoes, straightened his back and pursed his lips.

'Hello, hi!' he bellowed, cutting through all the noise. It stopped in an instant. 'I'm the Doctor. You are blessed and highly favoured by the Gardens of Kubuntu and crowned in the light of your ancestors' sun!' He smiled and raised his hand, bending his thumb as Mo had shown him earlier. After responding appropriately in unison, Fala, the Firebrand and Mya all raised their hands too.

'Wonderful! Now, I like liberation, big fan of it in fact, done a fair share of liberating myself, but violence, violence isn't my thing. Now you lot, the Yewa. You're all one people, your culture is vibrant and vivid. *So* vivid! The joy contained within this land has given me synaesthesia.' He sighed with relief. He was back, processing as normal... well, just about. 'Yeah. All my senses activated in tandem. I can actually taste feelings. What is that? Empathetic telekinesis heightened by the crystalline topography of the planet creating a feedback loop through the synapses connecting touch, taste, smell, sight and hearing? Ooh... heightened by the proximity to the Gardens maybe, the centre of life on Yewa.' He found himself a neutral position with Mya and the Gardens to his right and Fala, Ruby and the Firebrand to his left.

Everyone was still staring at him. Good. While they were staring at him they weren't attacking each other. Not yet.

'Now I have lived a long time, a very long time, and I have seen it all. Millions of beginnings and endings. And this situation here ends one way. Violence only leads to more violence, and all this will be destroyed.' He gestured at the beauty of the Gardens before him. 'Environment is a forgotten casualty of war. Now, I'm sure we all want a peaceful resolution to this conflict ...'

Fala scoffed. '"Peace" is the propaganda of our oppressors. We want freedom, we want justice,' she said, once again breaking rank to encroach on the Garden's perimeter. 'Mya, if you do not stop harbouring those fugitives, you leave us no choice. Violence is the only language they understand. They just attacked the Kaloa, the sacred festival. Just now, Mya. They surrounded your precious Nazari like hyenas. And you want to host more of them?'

The Doctor thought about making a joke about *The Lion King* to lighten the mood. *Time and place, Doctor, time and place.*

Mya was bristling. 'If you do this, Fala, you will start a war. Is that what you want – diplomatic blood on your hands? Have you consulted the ancestors? Would this make them proud?'

Fala's expression of defiance became one of pure fury. She spat at Mya's feet. 'Don't you dare. My... ancestors suffered at the hands of the Bia for many a generation.'

Mya sighed. 'Neither planet can afford this. I assure you the attackers you seek are not here—'

'I will raze this place to the ground to get the justice I want!' Fala barked.

The Doctor stepped towards Fala cautiously. He didn't know what to make of her. How much damage could one person do with an army of twenty? He could see so much of himself in Fala, her sense of moral conviction, her self-righteousness, her rage. He knew that any damage was too much and he knew how this story ended and wanted no part of reliving it.

'Let's just talk,' he said. 'Tell me exactly what you want. There has to be a way to resolve this without bloodshed.'

'Show me,' demanded Fala. 'Show me, Doctor!'

The Doctor was chilled to the bone. He felt her fury. It was white hot, and it overwhelmed him with paradoxical cold. Something again had shifted. He was more than used to having a heightened sense of awareness, and his default was to willingly drink in all the details of his surroundings. But today there was a hypersensitivity to even the intangible that became a distraction. There was so much noise, so much feeling, so much texture.

'We will not be moved,' said Fala defiantly.

RAT-A-TAT-TAT, RAT-A-TAT-TAT, RAT-A-TAT-TAT! The drums began again.

From the back a young Yewan protestor yelled, 'I will die before I am moved.'

The Doctor recognised the new arrival.

'Mo,' Ruby breathed, as the Yewan pushed through the fortified Firebrand forces, shooting a weapon into the sky.

'I will die before I am moved!' he yelled again.

For the first time, the air's temperature matched the icy appearance of the planet around them. Ruby looked down: she could see her breath. She watched as the vapour left her mouth and the molecules slowed down and came closer together to form tiny ice crystals.

'What the hell?' she muttered to herself.

Suddenly, from the ether appeared three malevolent, spectral creatures, shrouded in darkness.

'Can you see what you have done?' Mya cried. 'You know the Wraiths cannot be stopped! Run! Leave now!'

Ethereal and haunting, the Wraiths' shadowy figures phased by, disappearing into black mist and reappearing elsewhere in an instant. Each fresh apparition was coupled with chilling whispers in an ancient language Ruby could not decipher – which surely meant the TARDIS couldn't decipher it either.

She had an overwhelming sense of danger and leapt up to run towards the Doctor but was confronted by one of the figures, stopping her in her tracks.

Ruby willed herself to move, but couldn't. Her legs just wouldn't go.

A million unsaid goodbyes swam through her head in the seconds it took for the Wraith to reach out to her.

Ruby felt shooting pains in her lower back and palms. She was on the floor. Somebody had saved her, pushed her out of harm's way. She looked up and saw Mo standing in front of the Wraith. He spread his arms in acceptance of his fate and smiled. 'I become my ancestors.'

Ruby watched helplessly as the Wraith's long outstretched finger touched Mo's forehead. The process took all of one second, but Ruby somehow experienced every grotesque detail as if it were happening to her.

First, she felt all the colour drain from his body, his tattoos disappear and his once vibrant orange skin turn pale with dehydration.

Then she felt the tissues in his body shrink violently and collapse in on themselves.

Ruby scrambled to her feet just as the Wraith turned to face her again.

'Ruby! Over here!' the Doctor cried, attempting to get through the storm of protestors. But now white laser blasts were zipping through the air, as the protestors opened fire on the Wraiths. Finding no way through the blizzard of laser-fire, he turned to Mya. 'Turn the Wraiths off! Turn them off right now!'

'I can't, the defences are automated!' Mya was wringing her hands. 'They activate when they sense any violent threat to the Gardens. That young man set them off when he fired his phaser!'

The Doctor pulled out his sonic screwdriver and aimed it at the sky, trying to jam the security system's frequency.

Nothing.

He tried again, determined not to lose his friend. He attempted to jam the Firebrand weapons' frequency, hoping to protect her from unwitting crossfire.

'Can't get a fix,' he muttered, smacking the device against his hand in frustration.

Ruby now stood face to face with a Wraith.

Just as its outstretched finger met Ruby's forehead, Fala grabbed her by the hand, whisked her away and shot at the Wraith in one fell swoop. It disappeared into mist and then reappeared behind the Doctor.

He felt it behind him and spun to look at it. The Wraith had no visible facial features; it was like staring into a black hole.

Empty. No light, no life, nothing.

'I'm not a fan of this behaviour!' the Doctor told the Wraith as its long bony finger reached for his forehead. 'Why can't I find you? Why can't the sonic recognise you? There's so much noise...'

The Wraith seemed to hesitate. It lowered its finger and opened its shroud, enveloping the Doctor and Mya. The Doctor closed his eyes.

When he opened them again, Mya and he were both behind the resort gates. He felt warm... *A thermal teleport,* he thought to himself. *Strange, but no time for that now.*

He stared through the gates as the pandemonium beyond continued. Fala was pointing at Ruby. 'Take her!'

With military precision, Fala's followers formed a protective circle around Ruby, shooting at the Wraiths as they appeared and disappeared at unbelievable speed. Fala nicked one in the side and it collapsed in front of them.

At once, the remaining Wraiths stopped, fixing themselves firmly in reality, then split in two. There were now four of them surrounding Ruby, Fala and her followers. One by one they opened up their shrouds and flung their heads back.

'Cover your ears!' Fala instructed. Without hesitation her followers did so. She turned to Ruby and repeated emphatically, 'Cover your ears!'

Ruby complied just in time. An ear-splitting, high-frequency screech began to resonate from the Wraiths.

Helpless, the Doctor watched as tortured screams resounded from Ruby and the rest of the protestors. 'Ruby!' he yelled, desperately pulling at the metal gates over and over again. Ruby was writhing in agony. He could do nothing.

He saw Fala grab Ruby by the waist and pull her close. She was holding something – a small disc. She pressed it, and a hole appeared beneath them. *Vwoosh!* In an instant, Ruby and Fala disappeared through the ice. One by one the other protestors followed suit, vanishing through portals in the ground.

Telepads, must be, thought the Doctor. *Short-range transporters taking Ruby ... where?*

Again, he heaved at the gates, willing them to open with all his might. They wouldn't budge, and he turned to Mya. 'Open them up, open them up right now!'

'I'm sorry, Doctor, it's out of my hands. The gates are deadlocked after the Wraith systems activate. The whole resort perimeter is in lockdown.'

He turned to face the Wraith that had brought him and Mya behind the gates. 'Fetch Ruby!' he demanded.

The Wraith, its face – if it had one – lost in shadow, laughed at the Doctor. He could hear it in his mind, not his ears; a form of telepathic laughter that skipped past his cochlea and settled directly into his consciousness. It mocked him and dazed him. The Doctor gritted his teeth. His rational brain knew the Wraith hadn't taken Ruby; he had watched Fala rescue her. Even still, his gut told him they were to blame. And there it was again, that synaesthesia. He could taste his feelings: he was angry, scared, guilty, yet at the same time he felt relaxed, protected, warm and safe. The paradox of emotions made him even more frustrated. 'No, no, no. My friend has just been kidnapped, and you're ... laughing?' He stepped towards the Wraith. It disappeared and joined the rest on the other side.

'You have made an enemy of me today,' the Doctor informed them. 'I'm going to find my friend and then I'm coming back for you all.' The Wraiths watched the Doctor for a moment and then vanished, serially disappearing into a dark mist and then thin air.

Mya edged towards the Doctor. 'They're automated systems, you know. They can't laugh or even really hear you…'

The Doctor ignored her and began to walk towards the entrance of the resort. The path was lined with various plots belonging to different ecosystems, rare and exotic plants that all thrived under distinct climates. The tundra, the desert, tropical rainforest … and this was just the ground floor. The scientific engineering it must take to regulate such wildly different ecosystems in such close proximity was truly astounding, but the Doctor knew he had to focus. 'You know Fala. Where would she have taken Ruby?' he demanded.

'She will be safe with Fala,' said Mya. 'Trust me, she wouldn't hurt an innocent—'

'An innocent? This is the Fala who's baying for "violent liberation"!' Two large glass doors barred the Doctor's way, but with a flick of his sonic he opened them instantly. 'Typical,' he said. 'Are these under a different frequency?'

Mya nodded. 'These doors are brand new, about a week old. They have not yet been connected to the security systems.'

The doors slid open to reveal an opulent circular foyer adorned with a striking blend of white, purple and gold accents. The floor gleamed with polished marble tiles in shades of ivory and cream, subtly reflecting the glow of the grand chandelier overhead. Crafted from glistening white diamonds and gold-plated fixtures, the chandelier cast a warm and inviting light throughout the space.

Around the room's circumference, plush furnishings in rich shades of signature Yewan deep purple – velvet-upholstered armchairs and sofas – surrounded marble-topped coffee tables hosting delicate crystal sculptures and fresh floral arrangements in opulent vases.

Behind the desk were two more Wraiths, floating dormant.

Upon seeing them, the Doctor hesitated. 'Why didn't you kill me?' he demanded. Then he stopped; these Wraiths were different, identical in shape but white with gold accents. Their hoods hosted a faceless white void of endless bright light.

As Mya joined them behind the desk, they disappeared in a puff of white smoke.

'Those were dormant Wraiths,' she said. 'They only appear when a service desk is unmanned. They are basically just projections, Doctor.'

'Those projections were hurting people. Killing people! And it's on you.'

'I tried to stop Fala, I couldn't stop the Wraiths...' She looked pained but almost blank, as tired teachers do when class discipline is beyond their control and they are beyond caring. In that moment, the Doctor saw a woman who was just trying to do her job and thought better of making it any more difficult for her.

'I'm sorry,' he said more levelly. 'That's not me, the blame and shame thing. I feel... out of sorts. You know?'

'You are feeling something that belongs to someone else,' Mya said softly. 'You see, all Yewa are connected. We are a telepathic race. When we die, our bodies decay into crystal and our emotions and memory are preserved in the ice. Everything that ever existed or currently exists on Yewa always remains, and it connects us to one another as well as our planet. As I stand before you, I was once the ground that lies beneath your feet.'

Although the Doctor sincerely appreciated the beauty of the sentiment, it didn't make things any easier on his brain. There were too many voices, too many feelings. 'Guess it takes a bit of getting used to?'

'We are taught from birth to fine-tune our senses,' Mya said, tapping away at the monitor behind the desk. The Doctor watched as she slowly shifted into customer service mode, beaming overenthusiastically as she turned back to look at him. 'We will be on lockdown for at least an hour, but I assure you, she should be safe with my sister.'

'Your sister?'

'Allow me to introduce myself more formally. I am Mya, Keeper of the sacred Gardens of Kubuntu, our original ancestor. Fala is my twin.' She pulled out a scanner and pointed it at the Doctor. 'Ah, a Time Lord. In our many years, we have never had a Time Lord rest with us. Welcome!' She tilted her head. 'The Wraiths were trying to protect you, not kill you. They are an archaic system designed to protect the Gardens and its guests. Due to your exalted status as a Lord of Time, they must have assumed you were resting with us.' She looked back at her holoscreen. 'Oh. You *are* resting with us! I have found your booking: the Doctor and Ruby Sunday. Please be assured I will compensate you fully for the inconvenience of losing your companion and ask our staff to get in contact with the Firebrand.'

'I need to take a look at your systems,' said the Doctor, whipping out the faithful old psychic paper. 'I'm not just a Time Lord. I'm also Lord of the Intergalactic Board of Hotel Inspectors,' he said with maximum authority and conviction. 'I assume Ruby was taken into the catacombs and I need to find an access point.'

Mya's customer service face dropped and she reverted back to her earnest self, warm and comforting. 'Doctor, that paper is blank.'

'Blank? Oh. Yeah, well. S'pose telepathic species and psychic paper aren't really a good fit.' He pointed at the leatherbound card holder with a scolding finger. 'Get it together.'

'There is no need for trickery here. I am more than willing to help you find your friend. You are a guest here and I will provide you with whatever you wish.'

The Doctor relaxed a little.

'As I said,' Mya went on, 'we will be on lockdown for a minimum of an hour, and the Wraiths won't let you leave the building.' Mya stepped out from behind the desk and offered him a lozenge. 'A complimentary confection. For your stress, Doctor. It will help you hear your own voice.'

'Thank you,' he said as he popped it in his mouth. 'Give me twenty minutes and a couple of biscuits and I bet I could reroute the systems.'

'I will get someone to show you to the security base but I fear it will be of little to no use. There is no access to the catacombs from the Gardens. Kubuntu herself willed it so. She said that the bodies of the dead must not come into contact with the plants, a symbol of the living. The Wraiths are as old as the Gardens. They were here before me and will remain when I become my ancestors. They are sentient and run separately to the resort systems that were installed just before the building of the hotel. I assure you, there is no connection.'

'Hmm... I'm not too sure about that. I'd still like to check the systems.'

'Certainly, Doctor. When the lockdown is lifted, the security systems will become available. In the meantime, I give you my word that Ruby Sunday is safe with Fala.'

Mya handed the Doctor his room key and then flagged down a passing bellhop named Fran. He stood tall, though his height was mainly in his torso, whereas most Yewans the Doctor had seen had long legs. Fran shuffled over awkwardly, as if walking required deliberate thought at each step – lifting a foot, moving it forward and placing it carefully back down on the ground.

'Fran, show the Doctor to his room, and then to the resort security base as soon as the lockdown is lifted.'

Fran smiled and nodded. 'This way, sir.'

The Doctor followed him towards the glass elevator in the centre of the foyer. He laughed to himself, then decided to withhold his hilarious comments about Chocolate Rivers and Oompa Loompas, as he was fairly sure they wouldn't translate.

As he and Fran ascended, the Doctor could see the communal pools and noted to himself that there was a significant Bia population. In fact, he realised, they were all Bia. Maybe Fala was right: the attackers from earlier may well have been hiding in the resort.

The Gardens of Kubuntu truly were an opulent haven. He mused at the internal architecture, designed with meticulous attention to detail. The resort blended seamlessly into the surrounding natural beauty of the Gardens and subsequently the rest of Yewa. The views were stunning.

The Doctor made a promise to himself: once he found Ruby safe, they would both get into this elevator again and properly enjoy the serenity of this magnificent backdrop.

'We aim to immerse our guests in a world of unparalleled comfort, sophistication and indulgence,' Fran piped up out of the blue, as if he had just remembered how to talk. He continued, as if quoting sections from the employee manual under duress: 'From the moment a guest arrives, they are enveloped in an atmosphere of exclusivity and exquisite service.'

The Doctor turned to Fran, who was sweating profusely. The edges of his tattoos looked raw. 'What's wrong? Are you okay?'

'Fine, sir.' Fran stood hunched over, groaning in pain.

'Fran, no offence, but you don't look good. You look bad. Go home, you need a lie down or something.'

'Happens all the time when new tattoos are coming in, I'll be fine.' After a few moments, he managed a smile as he straightened his spine, in an attempt to look normal. 'Each guest is assigned a personal bellhop who waits on you hand and foot, sir. I can't go home, not yet.'

'I'll tip you the day's wages if you go home now!'

Fran simply shook his head, stepped off the lift at the top floor, and guided the Doctor to his room.

Upon entering, the Doctor promptly halted in the doorway. The suite was expansive, furnished with plush décor, high-thread-count linens and cutting-edge technology.

The Doctor chuckled as he walked in, exclaiming, 'It just doesn't stop!' He surveyed the room, pointing to his temples. 'Universal translator system – got it, don't need it!' His eyes scanned the holographic room and climate control panel approvingly. 'Holographic room and climate control panel – very nice indeed.' He moved on, delighted. 'Virtual reality entertainment system and an anti-mav bed – now that's more like it!'

His amazement grew as he noticed the private pool outside, connected to a river that snaked through the Gardens via a massive waterslide.

'Ruby is gonna love this!'

'I'll be right back for you in a moment, sir.'

'I thought we were going to the security systems,' the Doctor said.

'We shall, sir. If you will just wait here, sir, I will be right back as soon as the lockdown is lifted. We are asking all our premium guests to wait in their rooms or the exclusive lounge until we have finished our briefing.'

The Doctor knew that every moment spent waiting around for Mya or Fran to get their act together put Ruby in more danger. He opened his mouth as if to argue, but when he saw how Fran was still suffering he let his cheeks soften into a smile. 'That's absolutely fine.'

He watched as Fran stalked away uncomfortably. Then, after waiting a minute, the Doctor walked the length of the corridor back to the lift. It only had two buttons: the penthouse and the foyer. The Doctor attempted a trip back down to the foyer but the lift was deadlocked so the sonic could not frustrate the security. He decided to double back through a set of doors at the other end of the corridor and found himself in the softly lit serenity of the premium lounge.

It exuded elegance. Stylish décor, cosy seating arrangements and art that seemed to gently move, each abstract blob of colour like watching living cells under a microscope. Lining the far wall in front of the view of the city was a gourmet buffet accompanied by decanters full of fluids in a range of colours and decadent desserts.

The lounge was vast but practically deserted. Its sole inhabitants were three Bia men who sat in the corner around the fireplace.

'Hello, I'm the Doctor!'

Two of the men turned to him and smiled warmly. The first Bia was a stocky man, sporting a moustache and peacock-inspired satin kimono. He introduced himself lazily: 'I am Bia Can, this is Bia Toh.' He pointed idly to an equally stocky man who had fallen asleep on a chaise. 'We are the grand viziers of the High Court of Bia. This is His Highness—'

Before he could finish his sentence, the Bia man in the middle jumped up, grabbed a glass and shoved it forcefully into the Doctor's hand with a smile.

'I am Lori, Prince of the Bia, and you are the Doctor, Lord of Time. Have a drink, friend.' He held out a hand, bejewelled with a perfect moonstone ring on one finger. The Doctor shook with Lori, then turned his hand over to get a better look.

'Oh, they are beautiful.'

'Family heirloom.' Lori grinned, admiring his own fingers.

The Doctor smiled. Lori was a handsome, strapping young man full of light. He was a little nerdy but in a cute way. Tall, broad-shouldered but somehow slightly lanky too. His smile reminded the Doctor of his own, cheeky yet comforting.

'You've heard of me,' the Doctor half-flirted.

'Heard of you? My friend, I am your biggest fan! You were my elective at university on Bia.' Lori couldn't help himself and embraced the Doctor. He held on so tight the Doctor half-wondered if he would wrap his legs around him too, like a koala on a tree. Eventually Lori let go, blushing with mild embarrassment at the intensity of his fangirl moment. 'Sorry, it's just, no one is going to believe me back home when I tell them I met THE Doctor. Come sit, have a drink.'

The Doctor stared at the glass in his hand. 'I really have to be going and I don't really drink,' he said cautiously, not wanting to offend His Highness but equally remembering that the last thing he'd consumed on Yewa still had him hearing colours and tasting thoughts.

'Well, you don't have to drink it!' Lori took hold of the Doctor's index finger and placed it in the drink. In an instant the liquid disappeared, absorbed by his finger. Bia Can did the same.

'Come sit,' Lori repeated eagerly.

Without really thinking, the Doctor sat down. Lori, full of a slightly obsessive zeal for learning, leant forward to the Doctor. 'I have read all about you. You were my favourite superhero story growing up.'

The Doctor laughed involuntarily. He had never thought of himself as a superhero and had done a lot of work to erase himself from most of history. 'I'm just a traveller, here for a bit of a break,' he replied humbly.

Bia Can cozied further into his seat. 'Aah, so you've come to retire too.'

'Right so,' said Bia Toh agreeably, still half asleep. He had just woken up from his nap, and so shuffled in order to find another comfortable position in his chair. 'Makes a lot of sense. We retired some years ago too,' he yawned.

'Aaah, is that so?'

'Back on Bia we were overlords. Tiring work, that,' Bia Can continued. The Doctor must have made a disapproving face because all three men perked up to clarify. 'Not mean overlords, good ones. Don't look at us like that, we were benevolent leaders!'

'Not that any of that matters to them. Ingrates, the lot of them,' Bia Toh grumbled.

Lori stood up to interject, fearing his advisers had not painted themselves in the best light. 'They are in a sort of "forced retirement". They nurtured the people and they sort of…'

'Turned against us,' Bia Toh moaned.

Lori clarified. 'No, they just didn't need you any more. The Bia, like the Yewa, are a telepathic race. Our people would raise their voices to tell us what they needed. And now… we hear nothing.' Lori looked sad and, for the first time, the hopeful light that gleamed off of his smile disappeared.

'Now cast off, we rest within the Gardens like the lotus-eaters of old Earth,' Bia Toh said.

'We're wasting away!' Bia Can grumbled again.

Lori moved to sit closer to the Doctor. 'Come now, friends, many people would kill to not have to work. Be grateful to the ancestors. You have fulfilled your purpose and you have fulfilled it well.'

'I'm sure there are people on Yewa that could use your help,' said the Doctor. 'Maybe you just need to change the frequency you listen at.'

Bia Toh and Bia Can sat up slightly. They had clearly never even thought of that.

Lori smiled. 'I'll put it to Nazari at lunch today! She's going to love it.'

Nazari? That name was familiar to the Doctor but he couldn't quite place it. 'Who's Nazari?'

'She is my *taiwina*. Sort of like a twin flame.'

The Doctor took another absentminded sip. He had a follow-up question, but by the time he put down his drink he had forgotten it.

Lori continued: 'My twin flame in more of a sibling way. The cores of our two planets were birthed from the same supernova, and we are both direct descendants of those cores. In our oldest library, there is an ancient union ceremony – the Ijoa. It's meant to happen every year and is prophesied to bring prosperity to both our nations. Hasn't happened in years, but myself and Nazari decided to bring it back. For the culture.'

'Aah yes, I heard the story in the market earlier. Why so long?'

'No one knows, really. Well, that is what happens when your culture is driven by a folk tale. A story.' Lori laughed. 'The Bia are hard driven by scientific proof whilst our Yewan counterparts are slightly more song and dance.'

There it was again, that apathy to knowing. The Doctor opened his mouth to press for an answer but felt the desire to know leave him too.

Bia Can sat up slowly. 'The Ijoa is the only ceremony our two cultures share, a lifelong bond that is rooted in mutual care and sharing of cultural practices. The Bia and the Yewa will renew ourselves as one nation. Fortified in unity.' He paused, then smiled. 'It's more ceremonial than anything else but brilliant for business.'

'It's a glorified peace treaty ceremony for tourists and a waste of time,' Bia Toh said. 'Best part is the free hotel.'

The Doctor started to feel queasy. Pointing at his empty glass, he asked, 'What was that?'

'Pure water from the River Ratehs.' Lori nudged the Doctor in the ribs playfully. 'It's rumoured to wash all your cares away.'

'Makes sense.' The Doctor found the sick feeling had faded, leaving him as relaxed as when he'd first arrived. He felt so carefree he didn't particularly care about whatever the Bia had to say for themselves. However, he decided to be polite and pretended to listen anyway.

Lori smiled and shuffled even closer to the Doctor. 'The ceremony will take place here, in the Garden's inner sanctum. We've invited ambassadors and dignitaries from all over Chimandra. Also some old trade partners of the Bia. Good for business, like Bia Can said. They're on their way here today.'

'Tomorrow, Your Highness.'

'Tomorrow? Time really does slip away from you here, doesn't it,' Lori laughed.

'This will be a mark of unity that will hopefully restore the peace between our two nations,' said Bia Can. 'It has been touch and go for a couple of centuries.'

'And then you'll return to your people?' the Doctor asked.

'Myself and the Bia High Court will stay on for two and a half more years,' said Lori. 'The Ijoa is a five-year festival and tomorrow is the main event. We're halfway there!'

'There is nothing waiting for us at home anyway.' Bia Can perked up slightly. 'Still, service here is impeccable, dedicated staff anticipating and fulfilling your every need. Personalised concierge services, private butlers, world-class chefs. No effort has been spared. It's like having a me!' Bia Can laughed.

'Ooh and don't get me started on the atmosphere here, Doctor,' said Bia Toh. 'Back home we were practically genies. "Do this," "We need that," it was endless. This place crafts an atmosphere of relaxation and refinement, where every moment feels like an escape into a world of extravagance and sophistication. A well-deserved break, if you ask me.'

The Doctor frowned. From seeming out of sorts, the Bia now sounded like a walking commercial, a less pained version of Fran's advertisement.

Lori countered with a smile. 'Well-deserved indeed, my friends. But, like the Doctor said, new work could now await us here.'

'Yes, Your Highness.' Bia Can and Bia Toh both grabbed another glass of Ratehs water, toasted their leader and stuck their fingers in the drink.

Lori stood up to excuse himself. 'Nazari hates it when I'm late,' he said, shaking the Doctor's hand. 'I look forward to catching up with you, Doctor.' Lori said goodbyes to his advisers and then ambled away.

Something in the Doctor finally switched. He had been sitting here, chopping it up with the Bia whilst Ruby was still missing.

How could he forget?

He shot to his feet. 'Note to self, no more mindless consumption. At least not without giving it a onceover with the sonic first.' He tapped himself lightly on the head in an attempt to jump-start his brain.

Eureka! That was it, he was back again. He scanned the lounge for the exit Lori had taken. He had been here a lot longer than him, so could probably direct him towards the security systems or at least back to the foyer.

As the Doctor made a beeline for the door, Bia Can chirped up. 'You seem tense, Doctor. The spas offer rejuvenating treatments.'

'No thanks,' the Doctor said, eager to not be distracted any further.

'Or maybe you're just hungry? Gourmet restaurants on every floor with the galaxy's finest cuisine!' Bia Toh smiled.

'Try and check out the leisure centre; they have a golf course and an indoor beach,' Bia Can called after him, but the Doctor was already gone.

The men looked at each other and shrugged. Relaxing wasn't for everybody.

Five

A mile below the city, deep in the catacombs, Ruby found herself rooted to the ground, overwhelmed by a profound sense of paralysis. That sensation of being able to taste other people's feelings and emotions had returned. It was sickly sweet. It reminded her of one Halloween when she was a kid. Cherry, her gran, was conked out in bed, and her mum, Carla, was out. So, left virtually unsupervised with an entire bag of treats, she'd eaten the lot.

Ruby could feel the tension in her body; her muscles had begun to ache from holding the weight of her fear. Her eyes were wired shut; she didn't dare open them. She wondered: if she did, would she find herself in the afterlife? Was there even an afterlife? Her next movement could answer a billion-year-old question. Everything that went down with the Wraiths outside the gates had happened so fast she couldn't be sure if any of it was real. But she knew that if she opened her eyes, whatever was on the other side of her eyelids would become her reality and she was not prepared for that.

All of a sudden, Ruby felt a subtle warm sensation on her shoulder. It flowed down into her torso, her back and then her legs.

'You're going to need to open your eyes for this next bit,' Fala said as she moved her hand from Ruby's shoulder.

Ruby opened her eyes to find the rest of the Firebrand staring at her.

'Please don't kill me, I promise I'm nice,' pleaded Ruby, her anxious laugh attempting to mask the genuine terror she felt. Almost like a nervous tic, Ruby absentmindedly flashed a thumbs-up at Fala and the Firebrand.

They all tilted their heads to varying degrees, reflecting the amount of confusion they felt.

'I thought I was a goner. I suppose if you wanted me dead, you wouldn't have protected me, but that being said – sorry, I'm waffling, thank you for—'

'I'd put a hold on your gratitude for the time being,' said Fala. 'As of this moment you are officially a hostage of the Firebrand.'

Ruby gulped.

'I am yet to determine your usefulness to my agenda,' Fala told her. 'But rest assured, if need be I will use your life to advance our cause. Now, we must go.' Fala signalled to two of the Firebrand. 'Take her. There is no time to waste.'

Ruby didn't resist as her arms were grabbed and the Firebrand shepherded her after Fala. They walked for what felt like hours, moving seamlessly through the labyrinthine network of narrow corridors adorned with hieroglyphic markings that had been carved into the powdery walls.

They finally reached what Ruby supposed must be the Firebrand base. Apparently carved out from the catacombs, it was fully equipped with shared sleeping quarters, a small kitchen and dining area, even what looked like a ping-pong table.

As Fala tended to her soldiers and organised her combatants, Ruby wondered if she could possibly find her way back to the Doctor, or the TARDIS – or even just the smile of Tamotah, the friendly fruit vendor from the market.

She noticed a recess in the corner. It was fully stocked with food, water and medical supplies. One of the Firebrand members pressed a button on the keypad. With a crunch like stiff unused bones grinding, the shelves turned slowly to reveal an arsenal on the other side. Guns, grenades and other assorted weaponry.

'Very *Scooby-Doo*, that,' Ruby said to herself.

She turned to look at the Yewans huddling beneath their planet's surface. They were all so young – on average they couldn't be much older than her. Where were their families?

Just then Fala appeared behind her, making her jump. 'You scared the life out of me,' Ruby told her.

'Good.'

Ruby wasn't quite sure if she was joking. Fala never smiled; she barely moved her face if she wasn't talking. Fala held out a tray, with bread, a piece of fruit and a canister of water.

Out of courtesy, Ruby took them with a smile but decided against consuming any more sustenance until she was back with the Doctor.

Fala then left her side to stand on a table. Her company gathered around her as she spoke, her words echoing eerily off the carved rock.

'We lost a brave friend today,' she declaimed. 'Mo was murdered in the name of the liberation. We must grieve, we must honour his memory, but we must also fight in his name and in the name of the ancestors. This is our final chance. This is our final assault. Remember, the Firebrand fight for the freedom of Yewa and we will not be moved. We will burn the resort and all inside to the ground if we must. You have your orders.'

Abruptly she pointed at Ruby, who up till that moment had been minding her business in the corner. 'I will take responsibility for... the liability.'

'Thanks,' Ruby said sarcastically, as the Firebrand dispersed. She watched as the young Yewans around her began pulling weapons and duffel bags from crevices in the walls and from under tables and chairs. In that moment, it dawned on her: this was their actual life, fighting and violence was how they existed in their world. She soaked in the uncomfortable revelation of her extreme privilege in comparison.

Fala stepped down from the table and called a few of the younger Firebrand members over. 'You will stay here – if anything goes wrong, you are Yewa's last hope.'

She then turned to a young man seated at a series of screens and panels. Ruby figured it was some sort of control centre that monitored the resort. On screen, a three-dimensional blueprint of the upside-down pyramids rotated slowly.

'This is the final strategy,' Fala told him.

Ruby couldn't hear the exact plan but somehow she could feel the beat of it, cold and calculated, through the crystals. She watched as schematics of the resort flicked through scenario after scenario of destruction. In one version of events, the whole resort simply imploded.

The Doctor's in there and he doesn't know anything about this, Ruby thought to herself.

Something rose in her, from the depths of her gut: a fear so hot that it melted away all other thoughts and snapped her into focus.

'Fala,' she said. 'Please. I really need to get back to the resort.' Ruby blinked, and in the time it took to reopen her eyes, she was pressed up against a wall with a phaser to her neck and Fala towering over her. Ruby caught a glimpse of three Firebrand members who were also now pointing weapons in her direction.

'Oh, I'm sure you'd love that,' Fala said coldly. 'Luxury? Relaxation?' A sneer spread over her face. 'Well, I will get you back to your friend and then you and your Doctor will leave this planet immediately. Yewa is a place for Yewans only. From today, we are officially closed to the galaxy.'

Fala stepped away from Ruby, took a bottle of liquid clipped to her belt and pushed it into Ruby's hand.

Ruby looked at it suspiciously and then back at Fala. If Yewa was just a place for Yewans and Fala had promised she'd do anything to rid this planet of intruders, Ruby figured she couldn't be too careful.

'It's not poison.' Fala rolled her eyes and took a swig of the water. She then shifted her pointing finger to the systems in front of them. 'These are systems for power generation, air filtration, waste management; they even create sustainable resources which replicate the sacred Gardens for food production. However it's all artificial, like on the rest of planet. The blast doors and reinforced walls mean that sometimes the air down here doesn't filter out as well. It takes some getting used to, especially if you are not Yewan. The water and food will help acclimate you.'

Fala pointed to a nearby chair, encouraging Ruby to sit. She took a sip from her own jerry can then passed it to Ruby. 'See, not poison.'

Ruby raised it to her lips. She was parched. As she drank, she prayed this wouldn't be a repeat of Tamotah's spicy fruit skewers. They had her brain feeling like it had been doing the conga for 24 hours straight.

'We will get word to our people on the inside. The Doctor will know you are safe and we are bringing you back to him.'

Ruby's headache evaporated and another clear question took its place in her mind. 'Why doesn't the fresh air reach the rest of the surface?'

'The resort must remain at the perfect temperature all year round, so they regulate changing seasons and climate by pumping the excess to the city and into the catacombs. The Garden has enough oxygen to sustain the entire planet but they hoard it and store it. Then give us the waste.'

'They pump chemicals into the resting place of your ancestors? That can't be right. Someone should do something...' She broke off sheepishly. 'You're doing something.'

Ruby drank more water, trying desperately to dilute the sickly sweet taste in her mouth. She couldn't help but think about how many dead people surrounded her and, only slightly more importantly, how she could soon become one of them if Fala decided to have another mood swing. The more she drank, the easier it became. She couldn't shift the taste but she now had the mental capacity to put herself to good use.

What would the Doctor do? she thought to herself. Investigate, get to know the people.

'Is that why you're protesting?' Ruby asked. 'Because of the chemicals?'

Fala stood up and walked over to a wall littered with ancient runes and hieroglyphs. As she spoke, she pointed to the pictures as if telling Ruby a bedtime story.

'Kubuntu's descendants, alongside the Keepers of the Gardens, were the original guardians of this planet. That responsibility has trickled through the generations and fallen at the feet of Nazari as well as myself and Mya.'

'Hold on. You're an heir of Kubuntu?' Ruby asked, struggling to follow the complex family tree in front of her.

'No. As twins, Mya and I were joint Keeper of the Gardens,' Fala responded. 'Our ancestors were revered as eternals, hand-crafted by Kubuntu herself, and since the beginning of time they walked among the people. And so did the Bia. You were at the festival earlier, so you know the story.'

Ruby had forgotten about the marketplace; it felt like days ago now. So much had happened since then.

'I left to start the Firebrand when I learnt the truth,' said Fala.

One by one, members abandoned their preparations and joined Ruby, until Fala had a captive audience.

'What's the truth?' asked Ruby.

They all listened with such intent and focus; you could hear a pin drop. Fala pointed to another picture. 'Over time, Guardians from other planets arrived and they would be shown such hospitality; the Yewa would take them among the Gardens of Kubuntu and offer its herbs and plants to heal. Tortured by wars and famine, they would come to Yewa and be taken to the crystal caves and diamond farms to realign their energy, bringing them good luck and abundance. The Yewa would bathe them in the Ratehs river and watch healing take place in a matter of seconds.'

This was where the hieroglyphs ended, faded and scratched away by time. Fala turned back to face her people and continued her story.

'And then, one day, over 200 years ago, nobody knows when exactly, the Bia came for the Ijoa. Famine and drought had ravaged their planet; however, that year, a miracle happened. The Bia returned to their planet, and legend has it that the ceremony revitalised their lands. Then they returned the year after, and the year after that, abusing Yewan hospitality and taking over, building paradise for themselves in our sacred Gardens so they would have a place to rest at every Ijoa. They started coming more often, in between ceremonies, more and more frequently. They would invite other species who offered gifts as payment for their lodgings. Now the Yewa have lost access to their own land, crystal lakes and mineral springs. All the plants in the city have wasted into nothing. The Garden is our only remaining source of life.'

'So is this how you plan to get it back? By burning it to the ground? Making it implode?' Ruby looked at the Firebrand, who were now concealing weapons in their clothing. 'What good will any of this do?'

'We will plant again,' Fala said casually. 'Apologists will say the reinstitution of the Ijoa and reunion of the two spirits in Nazari and Lori will strengthen the Yewans' claim to Yewa. But I say it is a sacrilegious act of false allyship. The Bia will come in their masses and take everything. They act jolly but they are in truth wicked and ruthless. They loot our Gardens and we get nothing in return. You all saw how they attacked at the festival. This is not the first time, and neither will it be the last. It ends today.'

Fala sent the Firebrand back to their duties and sat down next to Ruby.

'What about your sister? What happens to all the people who get caught in the crossfire?' Ruby said.

'Ruby, this war did not just start today. I did not pull the notion of violent liberation from atoms. The Firebrand have been fighting for justice for years!' Fala shook her head. Her face was wrought with melancholy and vitriol. 'By inviting more self-entitled, self-proclaimed highborns, Yewans risk losing what little they have. We will make the Gardens a symbol of unrest.'

'Then no one will want to come any more and you get your Gardens back.'

'Each person here has weighed the cost. Yewa teaches them the meaning of life is to live and live well. But the quality of life has diminished and so has the very meaning of living. You can taste the death, right? It's sweet, is it not?'

Ruby did not know what to say, so she said nothing. She desperately wanted to form a clever argument that resulted in everybody winning, just like the Doctor would. Yet she couldn't help but sympathise with Fala. She had been there a few hours and seen the effect of the Bia on the locals.

'Once the guests arrive at the resort, they never leave. That's the nature of this planet. It's a drug and it sticks. Now the prince of Bia wishes to invite trade nations to a sacred ceremony. If the Ijoa attracts more races, we risk extinction. And that is the sacrifice – losing a few shrubs and a few good people or losing the connection to the land and each other. If we cannot access our Gardens, they will all die anyway.'

'Look, there may be another way,' said Ruby. 'If you can only find the Doctor, trust him, he'll—'

'I've told you,' said Fala, 'I will make sure you are returned to your Doctor. I will not make any further promises after that.'

Ruby nodded. That hope of getting out alive fuelled her.

Fala stopped and inhaled deeply and then fixed her eyes on Ruby's, a beautiful abyss. Most eyes had notes of other colours, a speck of brown here, a fleck of hazel there. But not Fala's. Her irises and pupils were the same colour. She exhaled in a way that made Ruby feel uncomfortable. 'I do make one promise more. I will strike down anyone who gets in my way. Anyone.'

Ruby knew she was talking about her. Fala may have saved her once but she would 100 per cent sacrifice her if it came to it. Ruby tried to hide her worry, if only from herself, but it was no use. She really didn't know how infiltrating a group of vigilantes, hell-bent on what sounded very much like a terrorist attack, would go.

Six

The Doctor caught up with Lori at the end of the corridor, just outside the lounge. Lori was standing at a dead end, apparently admiring his hands, until he turned to face the Doctor and greeted him with open arms and a welcoming grin. 'Ah, Doctor. Missed me already?'

Although the Doctor found him charming, he had regained some semblance of focus and was no longer willing to make small talk or engage in any banter until he had Ruby securely by his side. 'Nazari, she's okay?'

'Of course, why wouldn't she be?'

'There was an attack in the market today, at the Kaloa.'

'Ah... an attack... by whom?' Lori seemed relatively unfazed.

'Some masked Bia men. They attacked a very nice fellow called Mo earlier too.'

Lori nodded, as if the Doctor's additions had provided him a world of context. 'Bia terrorists – or vigilantes, depending on your point of view. I heard they had resurfaced.' His expression shifted from understanding to worry. 'Better find Nazari quick then,' he mumbled, mostly to himself.

'How did Nazari get back here?' the Doctor enquired.

Lori simply shrugged. 'I dunno. When they say Yewa is connected, it isn't just metaphorical. Shortcuts exist everywhere. Her family have access to tunnels no living person has seen.'

The Doctor nodded thoughtfully. 'If she managed to get in, I'm sure she knows a way for me to get out.'

Lori waved his room key at the plain wall and the entrance to another glass lift appeared. 'After you!' He held out his hand and, once the Doctor had taken it, guided him into the lift.

'Why don't you have personal security?'

Lori raised his eyebrows and laughed. 'There is no real need. My dear Doctor, I've been at Kubuntu for many years and no harm has come to me yet. These people didn't even have a word for murder until a couple of centuries ago.'

The Doctor watched as Lori pressed the button for the foyer. He had an idea. Without further hesitation, he began to take apart the elevator control panel. 'All elevators are controlled by a central security system, so if I can track this back ...'

Beep. Beep. Beep. The sonic screwdriver had a pulse.

'You're a genius, Doctor. Why, thank you, Doctor,' he said, congratulating himself. He turned on the spot, following the direction of the beeping as it got louder and faster.

They arrived on the ground floor, and Lori stepped out of the elevator with a confident swagger. The Doctor grabbed him by the hand, stopping him in his tracks. 'Wait! What about Fala and the Firebrand? Outside the gates, they seemed hell-bent on forcing you to leave. You could be in real danger. Ruby's with them too. I won't let her get hurt. I couldn't live with myself.'

Lori smiled empathetically. 'Their quarrel is not with me, not really anyway.' He let the Doctor's firm grip melt into an interlocking of fingers. His palm perfectly balanced against the Doctor's. 'It is with Nazari, and by the ancestors that woman is more than capable of handling herself,' he said, then nudged the Doctor in the ribs with playful insinuation. 'First time we met, I touched her arm without explicit permission and she threw me to the ground like a rag doll. I'll be absolutely fine and so will she! Both the Bia and the Firebrand are pests with toy guns and toy ammunition. I will convene with the High Court and Nazari to create a plan of action.'

In that moment, the Doctor couldn't help but feel frustrated, mostly with himself. He had ended up back where he started, with no real sense of how much time had passed, and had failed to learn anything that would bring him close to getting Ruby safe and back by his side. He had been distractedly chasing his tail, and it needed to stop now. He looked down at the beeping screwdriver, once again tracing its direction.

Lori grabbed the Doctor's hand and kissed it. With a wink, Lori bid him adieu and retreated in the direction of the reception hall.

Crash!

The Doctor spun to find the source of the sound that had so violently interrupted his train of thought.

In the centre of the foyer lay a jumble of overturned trays, spilled drinks and scattered food. Standing over the colourful mess of fruits, sandwiches and snacks strewn across the floor were two young porters arguing with a Bia guest.

'Watch where you're going!' snapped the Bia woman.

'Please watch where you're going, miss!' said one young porter.

'I am a Jade member of this resort, I can walk wherever I like,' she replied with intense passive aggression.

'This took eight hours to assemble,' the second young porter complained, trying to reassemble her now decimated hard work.

'You'll just have to make another one,' replied the first.

'Are you crazy? Have you absolutely lost it? There's no way I'm doing that,' she said, standing up to shove the other porter. 'You barely helped the first time.'

'Don't push me!'

The two young porters began to argue, pushing, shoving and pointing fingers.

The Doctor was torn. Should he break up the fight, follow Lori because he now had more questions, or find the security systems? Something caught his eye: the Light Wraith behind the desk was gaining some motion and, as it did so, its shroud began to darken.

Something clicked. Dormant Wraiths had endless white voids for faces, which were, in a lot of ways, more unnerving than the black holes of their more sinister counterparts. As the arguing continued, the white shroud became as dark as the Wraith he first encountered outside. They were almost identical.

The ancient whispers began to rattle around his brain again, this time twice as painful.

The Doctor made a choice.

'Hey! Hey! Hey! What's all this?' he asked as he physically separated the two staff members.

'Typical!' the Bia woman sneered again, her tone full of prejudice.

'What's that supposed to mean?' the first porter spat back.

The Bia woman's eyes swelled with crocodile tears, and she grabbed her arm in pain. She was clearly putting on a show for the Doctor and he knew it. 'I was minding my business and they crashed into me,' she moaned. 'Look, I have a bruise.'

The Doctor looked but couldn't see what she might be referring to.

'This is all your fault,' the first porter said, redirecting his energy to his colleague. 'I told you we should have gone the other way.'

'I swear by the ancestors, he's lying! And so is she!' the second porter said, pointing at the guest. 'She's a liar. That's the way the Bia are.'

'I must have learnt it from your father,' the Bia woman retorted, making a gesture that the Doctor deduced must have been some form of obscenity from the reaction of all present. To insult one's parentage on a world where your ancestors are your gods had to be a form of sacrilege, surely?

This could get messy.

The two porters lunged at the woman and, once again, the Doctor physically separated them. 'Tsk-tsk-tsk. Please, no one got hurt, no one died, so let it go ...' The Doctor raised his hands. 'I'm sure it was an accident.'

One of the porters opened his mouth to protest. Then he saw Mya marching towards them and instantly clammed up.

'What is the meaning of this?' Mya demanded. 'I told both of you to always use the staff pathways for catering. Clean this mess up now!' She maintained a balanced gentility in her tone of voice but the strength of her glare was enough to send shivers down the spines of its targets.

'Please, Mya, the staff pathways are still on lockdown. The lifts are up and running but ...' The first porter trailed off sheepishly, evading her stare.

Mya apologised to the guest, finished scolding the guilty-looking young porters and instructed them again to clean up the mess they'd made. She then turned to the Doctor wearily, with the longest shift of her life painted all over her face.

He recognised this extreme level of weariness in an instant. *The burden of working in hospitality is the same in every galaxy, I guess,* he thought to himself.

'So Doctor, any luck with the security systems? Usually they self-regulate, and the lockdown should have been lifted by now. I can't have staff using the foyer as their own personal wrestling rings.'

'I've not seen the security systems!' the Doctor said. 'Fran showed me to my room and then he left.'

'Strange…' Mya scanned the foyer for the bellhop, eager for him to explain himself. He was nowhere to be seen. 'I'll escort you myself, then.' She took off towards another plain wall in the foyer. The Doctor silenced his beeping screwdriver and followed her.

Mya marched along a complicated network of corridors to the security base. Left, left, right, left, right and left again. It wasn't a long walk; they arrived in less than a minute.

'Why would Fran take me all the way to the top floor, and not return after his briefing?' mused the Doctor. 'He did look awful, to be fair.'

'What briefing?' Mya shrugged, preoccupied with passing the base's multiple levels of security. 'Honestly, you can never get the help these days.'

She finished her last levels of security checks with a retinal scan and voice recognition. The doors slid open and brightness shone out of the room, taking them both by surprise. Sunlight gleamed through the skylight and reflected off the white surfaces of numerous computer systems.

The Doctor clapped his hands together and smiled. For the first time since his arrival, he felt like his old self, a man of action, not a passive bystander.

He used his psychic paper to grant him access to the entire resort, every nook and cranny. Then he plugged his sonic into a port and set the scanners to search the planet for signs of Ruby.

Since they had started travelling together, he had surreptitiously collected DNA, fingerprints and retina scans from her time in the TARDIS. He had thought that the more data he could collate, the easier it would be to find Ruby's birth mother. Information was power, after all.

He moved over to the biometric scanners. 'I'm setting your systems to constantly look for Ruby's unique physiological features and energy signatures… Mind you, blonde hair, blue eyes and approximately 5 foot 1 on a planet where dark hair, tanned skin and impressive height is the norm, she should stick out.'

'What are you doing now?' Mya asked as the Doctor glided from monitor to monitor.

'Fala and the Firebrand disappeared below the crystal, I'm assuming into the catacombs. Which, as I suspected, also run under the Gardens,' he said, pulling up a 3D schematic of the internal infrastructure of the resort and its environs.

'Yes but the catacombs stretch for thousands of miles. They could be anywhere under the city. And the shields around the Gardens block anyone from using teleports within and directly under the resort.'

'That explains why we landed so far away. The TARDIS likes to park well away from trouble,' the Doctor grumbled. 'So that means they would have to teleport away from the resort. But just because they can't get in, doesn't mean we can't get out.' He looked around. There were no security guards in the security base, not even a Light Wraith. The upper echelons of high-born societies from all over the universe came here to rest, and not a single guard manned the central security system. When he pressed Mya for a reason, she retreated into herself mournfully.

'The Wraiths are our only security. They are ancient and merciless and will hear no appeal. Since the dawn of life on Yewa, they have protected the Gardens and their inhabitants. When the resort was built, they evolved to protect its guests and staff. The risk of capital punishment to any who cross them, anyone who so much as disturbs the peace, is deterrent enough.' For a moment Mya went somewhere in her own mind, recalling the countless people she had seen turn to crystal at the hands of the Wraiths. 'Before even building the resort, our ancestors created holographic shields as invisible barriers that could repel or detain intruders. To protect the unwitting from the Wraiths.'

'Ah yes, I see. Telepathic encryption, advanced species recognition systems employing encrypted mental pathways that only authorised individuals can access.'

The Doctor turned back to the 3D schematic. It was so large the screen could hardly display everything at once. He started at the main entrance and scrolled through the lush landscaping and water features that had welcomed him into the building. He moved through the foyer, past the spacious and modern lobby with high ceilings and a reception desk. Past multiple accommodation buildings, amenities, spas and leisure facilities that had been arranged in a U-shape around the central garden. The extensive greenery and flowing rivers of crystal were breathtaking, even in holographic form. Artfully designed paths and bridges connected different areas of the resort.

But when he scrolled downwards, he found that all routes to the entrance of the catacombs had been blacked out.

'What's off limits down there?' he asked.

'That is the inner sanctum, the First Garden. Our most sacred ground. Kubuntu planted it herself, and that is where the Ijoa will take place tomorrow. No one has entered for 200 years.'

The Doctor nodded, preoccupied as he tapped away at the computer. He was trying to hack the systems, to find a way into the catacombs, but was met with firewall after firewall. He sat back in a huff.

'Hmm... I can see the Wraith system online but dormant. Clearly, the original architects of the base could only get as far as monitoring their status but not controlling them. Wraiths have free will. Well, good for them, I guess. I'm updating your nano-surveillance swarms to update me directly through the sonic if there's any matter transference from teleports. The holographic shields are also online. I assume they work in tandem with the telepathic encryption. But there is a third one, a third security device I can't—'

The Doctor suddenly flung his head back and arms up with animated incredulity. 'Oh, how could I have been so stupid! Doctor, Doctor, Doctor,' he said shaking his head in self-reproach. 'It's this planet, it's making me slow, making me miss the obvious. The perimeter deadlock is lifted, so I could simply walk out now. If I could get an energy scan of the leftover matter transference from the Firebrand's teleport, I could reverse-engineer the signal to create a path for the TARDIS to follow. Like Hansel and Gretel with the gingerbread crumbs!' He turned to face Mya, who hadn't moved or said anything much. 'I realise that won't translate, but you get the gist.'

'No, Hansel and Gretel with the witch and the candy, I know of it,' the distracted Mya mumbled vaguely. 'Very clever, Doctor.'

The Doctor stopped and walked over to her, putting a reassuring hand on her shoulder like she had for him earlier. 'What's wrong?'

'It's nothing,' she said.

The Doctor saw her make a deliberate effort to perk up and plaster her customer service persona back on. He squeezed her shoulder gently and, at his affirming touch, Mya crumpled into tears. 'Hey!' He wiped gently at the wetness on her face. 'What is it?'

'I'm losing it, I'm losing it all. My job, my purpose, my love. The resort is falling apart, there is always something. An argument between guests, internal fighting among the workforce, an accident here, missing staff there, Wraiths threatening locals. The Gardens are dying.' She caught her breath and pressed a button.

The schematic turned 180 degrees to reveal row after row of dead plants in one of the middle tiers. 'It's spreading, faster than ever. I don't know what to do. I have done everything in my power – but nothing.' She wiped her face and sat down on the floor as if the weight of her overwhelming sea of emotion had worn her out. 'And the worst part is knowing your beloved planet is doomed and your love will waste it engaging in futile politics ...'

'Your love?' the Doctor encouraged her, sensing there was more to come.

'Nazari is – well, was – my best friend.' Mya looked downcast. 'And well ... at one point ... my fiancée.'

The Doctor's mouth dropped open. 'Really!' he gasped.

Mya took a deep breath. 'We had plans to elope, leave our lives here behind and start new ones far away. Our birthrights had become heavy burdens. Keeper of the Gardens used to be a sacred role, but now it's reduced to complaint management and fighting endless fires, literally and figuratively. I understand why Fala abandoned it. I wanted to as well. The pressure is unbearable, and the thanks are non-existent. Everything was set for our departure, but Nazari broke it off. Lori had come to her with a solution. He said that bringing back the tradition of the Ijoa might heal the dying Gardens, the way it had for the Bia so long ago, long before the existence of the resort itself. He said the two planets were born of the same core. The Ijoa is a celebration of that sacred bond; when we are united, our worlds find natural balance and restoration. The night before we were due to leave, she came to me. She had to honour her duty to Yewa, we both did. I think something is off, but the Ijoa is the only way to communicate with the ancestors directly. So I agreed.'

An involuntary tear formed in the Doctor's eye. It was a story as old as time, one he had lived and relived countless times. An impossible choice. Love or duty? Was it better to have loved and lost than never to have loved at all? He didn't know. He had lived thousands of years and was no closer to having an answer.

'It all happened so quickly...' Mya sighed. 'One minute we're together, the next she's bound to someone else for eternity.'

'I'm sorry.' He didn't have much more than that. He really wished he did.

'I am fine. I feel like my soul has been ripped out of my chest but I'm fine. I am also duty-bound to serve the Garden, which means serving the guests, including Lori and the Bia High Court, and so I will do. Nazari is truly the bravest woman I have met. I had given up. Honestly, I had done everything I could, but she reminded me that to worry idly without action is to sin against our ancestors. And soon, I will be able to talk to them – face to face. So, as Nazari has done, I also do: I put my soul aside and do what I must.' The meaning of the words had clearly escaped her but she was too heartbroken to think of making any real sense.

Beep! Beep! Beep!

Alarms were suddenly blaring throughout the security base.

The Doctor jumped to his feet and scanned the screens to find the source. The reception hall. An argument had broken out between Fran and the Bia High Court. There was no audio, but Fran was screaming at Bia Can, Bia Toh, Lori and the other Bia guests.

Without hesitation, the Doctor tore out of the security base and made a right towards the foyer, with Mya hot on his heels.

'No Doctor, this way! There's a shortcut.' She grabbed his hand and pulled him down another complicated set of twisting corridors.

The Doctor frowned. He was more used to being the hand-holder rather than hand-holdee.

When they arrived outside the reception hall, the Doctor attempted to push open the doors. They didn't budge. Mya tried her keycard and then the Doctor did the same with the sonic. Neither worked. From the other side of the door, they could hear yelling and crashing.

'Stand back,' the Doctor commanded. 'I've always wanted to do this.' He took three large steps back and then bounded towards the door, shoulder first.

The doors burst open and he looked around at the aftermath of chaos. In the minute it had taken them to arrive, the reception room that had previously matched the elegance of the rest of the resort had disintegrated into complete disarray. Sofas had been overturned, their cushions strewn across the floor; tables lay on their sides among shattered crockery and glassware. Paintings that once adorned the mighty walls hung crookedly, torn or knocked off their mounts completely. Ice sculptures and plant pots lay toppled, their delicate forms chipped and broken, their former beauty marred by the disruption.

In the midst of the bedlam, Lori, Bia Can and Bia Toh were confronting Fran. A woman stood between the two opposing parties, beautiful in a way that radiated from the inside and out. The Doctor could feel her soul from across the room: it was pure light, pure stardust, pure magic.

'Nazari!' Mya rushed to the woman and, there and then, the Doctor fully understood the depth of Mya's loss.

Nazari smiled awkwardly at seeing her ex, her tattoos gleaming brighter the closer she got to her.

An eerie stillness lay in the air, thick and stagnant; the Doctor could taste it, like bleach. In the centre of the chaos lay a man. Fran stood over the body, pointing a weapon at Bia Toh and Bia Can. He shot a white laser pulse into the air and then aimed it back at its original targets.

Lori stepped slowly in front of his viziers, using his body to protect them.

'What's happened to the defences?' Mya looked around helplessly. 'Where are the Wraiths?'

'Hey Fran, hey, what's all this? What happened?' the Doctor asked as he edged closer towards him.

'They killed him! They killed him!' Fran yelled, fighting back tears. 'Bia Can and Bia Toh.'

'We did no such thing, I've never seen this man in my life.' Bia Can looked both genuinely confused and offended by the accusations that had fallen at his feet.

'Nor have I.' Bia Toh shook his head in indignation.

'Step aside, Your Highness,' Fran said to Lori. 'My quarrel is not with you.'

'You know I cannot do that, my friend. Fran, was it?' Lori said softly, mirroring the Doctor's gentle steps. Fran nodded, wiping his tears with his hand. He still looked raw, quaking in pain.

'We did no such thing,' Bia Can protested again. 'I've never killed a man in my life.'

Lori waved his court into silent submission and then returned his attention to Fran. 'Lower your weapon, Fran. Let us all talk about this. Why do you accuse my court? Who is this man?'

The Doctor looked at the dead man's face and then Fran's. 'Is this... your brother?' he asked. The two men's faces were near enough identical.

Fran began to sob again. 'I let him return to his original state, with his ancestors,' he said solemnly before shooting the man on the floor in the chest.

The Doctor watched helplessly as Fran's brother's corpse collapsed in on itself. There was something familiar about that, the Doctor thought to himself. He had seen it before... But there was too much noise, too much going on.

'*They* killed him,' Fran yelled suddenly, firing his weapon at Bia Can, narrowly missing his head. Fran spun round, waving the weapon dangerously. 'And now the rest of you will join him if you come any closer.' He looked at Lori apologetically, 'I'm sorry, Your Highness.' Fran pulled out a telepad and pressed the button.

'That won't work here,' the Doctor said.

Fran scoffed. 'I have friends in high places, Doctor. Bia Can, Bia Toh, you will come with me or you will die.'

'I'm not going anywhere with you,' Bia Toh snarled.

'This is not the way to resolve this,' the Doctor continued, still creeping slowly towards Fran. 'Why does no one listen to me?'

'He's one man. Let the Wraiths take him,' Bia Can yawned.

'Where are they?' Mya said again, more emphatically, her distress clearly growing. She went over to a control panel to investigate.

'I have asked once, I will not be asking again,' Fran said.

'Come on, let's be reasonable,' Lori pleaded.

BOOM! BOOM! BOOM!

Smoke filled the room, and the guests scattered, screaming and wailing.

Once the Doctor had found his bearings in the pandemonium, he saw three Bia men, all armed, surrounding Lori, Bia Can and Bia Toh. They looked just like the Bia that had attacked Mo and the revellers in the market earlier.

'We will not grant you the luxury of leisure at our expense any longer,' Fran spat. 'Take aim!'

The Doctor pointed his sonic at a nearby vase.

SMASH.

The small explosion was just enough of a distraction.

'Take cover!' Lori instructed. He darted past one Bia vigilante, somersaulted and made a beeline for Nazari whilst Bia Can and Bia Toh split.

'Fire!' Fran instructed. The vigilantes opened fire. Fran's first shot hit Bia Can and he turned into shards of crystal. At Bia Can's death, every single plant within the vicinity died instantly – turning into small piles of crystal.

Mya stopped investigating the control panel and let out a scream. 'Stop this, the dead and the living must not come into contact. You will kill the Gardens. You will kill us all.'

The Doctor pointed his sonic to the sky, jamming the weapons of the Bia terrorists. Mya, Lori and Nazari sprang into action, dodging, weaving and ushering the remaining guests out of harm's way whilst the Bia insurgents smacked their guns in an attempt to get them working. The Doctor ran at Fran, tackled him to the ground and wrestled the telepad from his grasp. He pointed the sonic at it, reversed its polarity and pressed the button. One by one, Fran and his syndicate vanished the same way they had come, back through the ground.

The Doctor inspected the device. 'Thermal teleport … but it isn't warm. But how can they have come through the crystal? And where are the wraiths? How did these lot get past the Garden's defences?' Too many questions, not enough answers. Something was afoot. 'I need to get back to the security systems,' he muttered as he left the chaos of the reception room behind him.

Mya marched quickly after him. 'This is impossible. The control panel was fine. No alerts. This is not possible!'

'Doctor, wait,' said Lori. 'Bia Can was my friend. I want to get to the bottom of this.'

'No,' Mya snapped. 'Forgive me, but I must confine everyone to their rooms until the Doctor has an answer for us.' She turned and instructed her staff to escort everyone back to their suites. 'No one is to leave unless I say so.'

Before Mya could follow the Doctor, Nazari grabbed her by the hand and pulled her back. 'You be careful, my love,' she said warmly.

Mya fought back tears and looked away.

'Mya... no matter what, you will always be—'

'I can't hear it... not now. Please, Nazari, not now.'

She gently eased her hand out of Nazari's, smiled despite her stinging eyes, and walked away.

As Mya disappeared round the corner, Nazari's tattoos faded until they were just light grey markings on her skin.

Seven

Ruby watched from the back as Fala's forces lined up in the catacombs. They were dressed like various resort staff: gardeners, waiters, bellhops, cleaners. No two people had the same disguise.

Fala rolled her shoulders back and stood tall. 'We have word, the defences are down. You have your assignments. Do not fail.' She turned to Ruby. 'We don't have enough telepads, so you will have to ride with me.' Fala took her hand and placed it on her shoulder.

Just then a young woman burst through the corridor and broke past the Firebrand ranks to stand face to face with Fala. She was out of breath, gasping for air.

'Fala, I have just heard! The Bia attacked the resort. Our people on the inside are warning us, it will be too dangerous to attempt—'

Fala put up a hand to stop her in her tracks. 'We know the danger. Our plan must go ahead. The Bia attacking is a good thing – more chaos for the Gardens, more cover for us. They won't be prepared for another attack so soon.'

'But Fala, there is a man, her friend.' The young woman pointed at Ruby with a violent air of accusation. 'He is tightening security measures as we speak. There is no way we can all go now without being detected instantly.' Fala stared at the young woman for a moment, then scanned the faces of her followers. Eventually she closed her eyes and lifted her head towards the surface.

The whites of Fala's eyes disappeared, consumed by a black mist that seeped out of her pupils. Ruby took a cautious step back towards the wall. She could hear ancient whispers coming from the walls. Or at least that was what she felt. Inside her head: *BE ALERT! WAKE UP! THEY ARE NEAR!*

Fala inhaled deeply, and her eyes returned to normal. 'I have consulted with the ancestors. I will go ahead … with the hostage.'

Ruby shifted awkwardly. *You never get used to being called that*, she thought to herself.

'I will infiltrate as planned and deactivate the systems again.' Fala was still addressing her forces. 'Stay vigilant. On my signal, you will join me. Ruby, despite this, I will honour our agreement.'

Something had been bugging Ruby. Fala and the Firebrand had made no attempts to conceal their identities or even their plan. And they were just going to let her go? She knew she shouldn't ask, she begged herself not to. *Don't say it don't say it don't say it.*

'Why are you revealing your whole plan to me? How can you be sure that I won't just—'

'I have waited for too long, far longer than you or the Firebrand can ever imagine. I will not let anything or anyone get in my way.' Fala calibrated the telepad and repositioned Ruby's hand on her shoulder. 'You tell your Doctor whatever you like. He will not be able to stop us. And bloodshed is inevitable. It is your choice whether you add your own to the spillage.' Fala smiled. She spoke warmly, but it couldn't mask the threat beneath her grin.

Ruby gulped, nodded and smiled too. It was a unique form of self-defence. There was nothing she could do now, but that wouldn't stop her from telling the Doctor everything.

Fala's fingers danced over the telepad, its screen casting an eerie glow on her face. She activated the small disc, and the telepad hummed to life with a low, resonant thrum. Its surface began to shimmer, emanating a gentle warmth that gradually intensified. The air around them began to distort. Ruby could see the heat waves. The waves vibrated more and more until they created a field that enveloped them both.

Fala put her hand on Ruby's shoulder. Her eyes held a steely glint that sent a shiver down Ruby's spine. Ruby's heart pounded madly, her mind racing with a thousand thoughts of ways to escape and warn the Doctor.

Within moments, with a soundless pulse, Fala's form became translucent, her edges blurring as if melting into the air. Ruby looked down and saw the same was happening to her. The surrounding area briefly flickered with an intense burst of heat, and then, in the blink of an eye, they vanished.

The next thing Ruby knew, she was standing at a delivery entrance at the rear of the resort. She assumed it was the back because nothing about it was familiar. There were no plants, or rivers, just an endless plane of ice, thickly layered with dunes of crystal flakes. It could have been a desert.

She stood behind Fala as they were greeted by a shady, masked individual. 'We must be quick. I have no idea when the systems will be back and the others...' He looked past Fala at Ruby and trailed off.

Fala quickly interjected. 'Never mind her, she is none of your concern. Move.' She turned him round and pushed him in his back.

With Ruby in tow, Fala's insider infiltrated the defenceless Gardens through the staff pathways. They came to a fork in the corridor and parted ways with the man who had let them in. Fala took a few steps, stopped and turned.

'Now, what to do with you?'

'You're in now, that's what you wanted, right? You don't need to "do" anything,' Ruby bumbled hopelessly.

Fala took her in. 'You're very... nice.'

'Thank you'

'I hate nice.'

Fala grabbed Ruby by the throat, forcing her against the wall. Her hand was hot and clammy, but the grip was weak, as if she could barely hold on. Ruby looked up at Fala, noticing the beads of sweat trickling down her significantly paler face. Seizing the opportunity, Ruby mustered all her strength and pushed Fala away, sending her crashing against the opposite wall. Without a second thought, Ruby bolted down the labyrinthine corridors, never looking back. She sprinted through the maze of labelled hallways – 'KITCHEN', 'SPA', 'GAMES ROOM' – until she spotted one that read 'FOYER'. She darted towards what appeared to be a dead end, praying for a miracle.

As she drew closer, a door materialised and slid open, revealing an empty foyer. Ruby stepped inside, sighs of relief tumbling out of her.

Now find the Doctor, Ruby thought, still recovering from the chaos. She looked around; the place was completely deserted. Not a guest or even a staff member in sight. She ran over to the front desk and rang the bell repeatedly.

Ding ding ding ding ding.

'Time for a full diagnostic!' the Doctor told Mya as he reset the defences in the security base.

'I don't understand what's going on,' said Mya. She looked weary and out of sorts. 'The Wraiths aren't protecting, teleports that shouldn't be able to function have been working just the same...'

'I know. None of this makes sense.' The Doctor loved puzzles but hated games. He felt like he was being toyed with, but the challenger wasn't playing fair. Like they had hidden the corner pieces of the jigsaw. '200 years ago, something real bad goes down between the Bia and Yewa – no one knows what, no one seems interested in knowing why, which is interesting. I digress. Point is, everyone is more than happy to be at odds – that's big bright red flag number one. Then we have the defences: sometimes they work, sometimes they don't – red flag number two. Then we have the dying Gardens – and that makes three. With the added layer of mayhem that is Fala and Fran, constantly firing weapons—'

Bloop. The systems diagnostic was complete.

'Look here.' The Doctor beckoned Mya closer. 'Fran overrode the Gardens' defence systems to teleport the rest of the Bia vigilantes past its protective forcefield.'

Mya looked shocked. 'That is impossible. Fran could not have accessed the systems. They are biometrically locked against all staff for this very reason.'

'Okay, so how? And when? We were here. We were both here.'

'I'm at a loss.'

'And why? Right back to the source.' The Doctor typed away. 'Hmmm, that's odd. These logs only go back 200 years. Can you think of a reason why? How old is the resort?'

Mya looked up pensively. 'I'm not exactly sure. But Lori, Bia Toh and Bia Can first arrived around that time, according to the logs.' The Doctor must have made a face because Mya's follow-up answered his unspoken question. 'The lifespan of the average Bia is longer than most. Their advanced technology allows for slower ageing.'

The Doctor pointed his sonic screwdriver at the screens in front of him. 'No, no, no! Only 200 years. There has to be more information. This can't be it. The Wraiths are sentient, right? They have been here since the beginning? Maybe we can rig up a rudimentary communication system. Do they only work on the perimeter?'

Before he could finish his questions, the alarm blared obnoxiously again.

BREHN! BREHN! BREHN!

'Ancestors, let me join you,' Mya huffed. She looked thoroughly fed up. 'What now?'

The Doctor empathised with her – she couldn't catch a break. Once again, he scanned the monitors for the source of the threat. There it was, in the foyer: Ruby! He smiled.

'You clever thing!' He rushed towards the exit.

'Oh no, oh no, oh no,' Mya burbled.

The Doctor stopped in his tracks and spun round. 'What? What is it?'

She pointed at the screen. 'Those are the Wraith alarms.'

No such alarm rang for Ruby in the foyer. She frantically poked around behind the desk and found herself aimlessly pressing buttons, anxiously looking over her shoulder in case Fala had decided to return her to hostage status. 'Mirror, mirror on the wall,' she begged the screen. 'Tell me where the Doctor is, pretty please and thank you.' Blissfully unaware, she continued her haphazard attempts at navigating the computer systems. 'Hello, hello! Doctor! Mya! Anyone?' Ruby called out.

Suddenly, the temperature inside the foyer dropped drastically. Time slowed. Ruby could feel her blood vessels constrict and the hairs on her arms stand on end. She ran her fingers over her goosebumps and watched as her hands turned blue. Slowly a black mist formed in front of her and in it appeared a Wraith. Just one. Larger than before, darker too. Ruby's entire body was overrun with pins and needles. It wasn't just uncomfortable, it was painful. The Wraith moved closer, and time returned to its typical tempo.

Ruby made a break for the elevator but, before she could reach it, the Wraith blocked her exit. It toyed with her, appearing and disappearing at her every turn. She found herself backed into the corner. As it crept in closer, she screamed, 'DOCTOR! DOCTOR, CAN YOU HEAR ME?'

The Wraith laughed. She could hear it mocking her: it mimicked her voice, but added a childish sing-song overlay.

Doctor, Doctor, can you hear me.

'Oi,' said Ruby, 'I don't sound like that!'

The Wraith continued its maniacal laughter.

It whispered again in their ancient language; it was different from the one in the catacombs. Only slightly, like two dialects born from the same root language.

Ruby Sunday, the girl abandoned, the girl who will now die alone.

Ruby knew this wasn't true. She may have been about to die, but she knew she was loved and she knew she was cared for, and that was more than enough for her.

Are you scared? We don't need your fear. We need your anger, your rage.

'Well! You know nothing about me, who I am or where I came from! You know nothing about my mum or my gran! You are—'

Ah, there it is.

The Wraith tripled in size and grew so dark, there were no edges or ridges to be seen.

Pure darkness. Closing in.

Just then the Doctor whizzed past! He vaulted Mya's desk and grabbed the monitor. The sonic was already in his hand. He pointed it at Ruby and then the screen.

'She's now staff, so away you go,' he said triumphantly.

The Wraith continued to edge towards Ruby. She drew one last breath as it raised its long bony finger to her forehead, and then ... it vanished.

Ruby exhaled in such a way that her whole body deflated, and she sank to the floor. Before she could finish her descent, the Doctor rushed over to her and folded her into a massive hug.

Overcome with joy, he swung her around a few times before gently setting her down. She was cold to the touch.

'I'm so sorry I didn't find you,' he said, and dropped his head, as if avoiding her gaze.

Ruby was having none of that. She lifted his chin to make sure he met her eyes. 'Hey, I'm fine, I'm safe. That's all that matters. OMG I have so much to catch you up on!'

The Doctor smiled. 'Me too! But first, do you want to see our suite?'

Eight

Shortly afterwards, Ruby found herself sat in the middle of an emperor-sized bed, nestled comfortably into the softest robe she had ever experienced in her life. She sank herself as deep as she could into the marshmallowy sheets, thriving in their warm embrace.

But guilt nipped at her. 'Doctor, are you sure we shouldn't we be out there, stopping Fala and doing... I don't know, *something?*'

'Usually, yes, but today – no. I think we need the quiet. I think the constant chaos is key to whatever is going on here. Every time we're close to an answer – BOOM, someone adds another question.' The Doctor paused, and sonicked the small buffet from room service on the trolley beside her. 'We should eat,' he decided. 'Shouldn't have too many adverse side-effects now that you've been here for long enough... I think.'

Without further delay, Ruby tucked in. Besides Tamotah's fruit stick, she hadn't eaten anything today. The chefs had managed to rustle up some human delicacies for her, no effort spared.

It was evident that there was little to no cohesion in the kitchen as the buffet featured delicacies from all over Earth. It was as if they had simply googled 'top Earth food' and hoped for the best. Ruby panned over the spread, searching for something familiar. She wasn't a particularly picky eater but had endured enough surprises for the day. Her eyes landed on a patty labelled 'chicken'. The yellow flaky pastry pocket crumbled in her fingers. She took a massive bite and chewed through the firework display occurring in her mouth. 'Mm, tastes like home,' she sighed, full of contentment. 'You sure you don't want a bite? There's more than enough for me,' she said, holding out the half-eaten pastry to the Doctor, who was anxiously patrolling the perimeter of the room. 'You're pacing again.'

'Yes. Pacing is good. Pacing gets the blood flowing. Flowing to the brain. Okay, let's recap … slowly.'

Ruby sat up, ready to engage meaningfully.

'So, you and I, we land on the most peaceful place in the galaxy,' the Doctor began. 'A place supposedly so peaceful that the most powerful people don't have private security, there are no authorities, and they only learnt the word for murder a century or two ago.'

'Right. And since we landed, it's been absolute madness,' Ruby put in. She squinted at the Doctor. This was a pattern for him. They'd whizz off to faraway distant lands and, wherever they ended up, there was some mystery to solve or some adventure to embark on. She loved it. Never a Tuesday or a February with him, only Friday nights and summer fun.

'Yes, chaos and mayhem, just a complete lack of order and structure. The Bia vigilantes attack Mo in the market and then Nazari. But why? According to Mo, "that's just the way the Bia are", but no – there must be something else. Things never just are, things are always things. With meaning and purpose. So, then those same vigilantes manage to bypass the security systems and attack the Bia High Court with Fran. Fran then accuses them of killing his brother, but they claim otherwise… and I believe them, I dunno why. Fran then commits murder in front of a roomful of nobility which is, by all measures, an absolutely crazy thing to do. He must have been desperate.'

'Right. And who's Fran?'

'He was our bellhop. The security systems said he overrode them and let the rest of the Bia teleport in. But he couldn't have unless he had remote access to the security systems, and he doesn't. And because I haven't figured out how, they could easily do it again and finish what they started. Mya has Bia Toh on constant watch. Anyone who commits an assassination in plain view of witnesses is unlikely to stop if the job wasn't done.'

'Fala and I got in because she has people on the inside who told us the systems were down and we could slip in under the radar,' Ruby told him. 'Some guy let us in. I couldn't see his face – he was deffo Yewan… maybe if I saw his tattoos again…' She shrugged apologetically. She hadn't been much help.

'Why didn't she mount a full assault as planned?'

'Because one of the Firebrand also got word that you were heading back to the security base so it would be too dangerous for them to all come through at once.' Ruby stopped snacking and looked up at the Doctor. 'Fala is dead set on justice and will stop at nothing. And she made me promise that we would leave right away.'

'Can't do that, Rubes, there's another mole – or multiple moles – and this lot need our help. We need to get to Fala before she can get her reinforcements through. If the Bia and Fala meet head to head, there is no telling the amount of trouble they'll cause. Every death causes the plants to die and this is the only source of oxygen on the entire planet.'

'So any conflict here means the death of this planet.'

'A whole race, suffocating to death,' said the Doctor solemnly.

'The problem is this place is massive. That bathroom is bigger than my entire flat…'

As Ruby spoke, the Doctor abruptly stopped pacing and grabbed his sonic screwdriver. 'I need a remote way to track the security systems.' He had always been an inventive DIY enthusiast and found himself on a mission to create a makeshift security system relay. He surveyed the room for potential components. 'What's getting me is, what do they want? Fran accused the Bia High Court of murdering his brother, but the Bia vigilantes also attacked Mo and Nazari in the market then paid no mind to her just now. What does all that mean? What is any of this in aid of?'

'Well, Fala wants all non-Yewans gone, and she is planning to do anything she can to stop the Ijoa tomorrow and make sure the guests don't come,' Ruby said, returning her attention to her feast.

The Doctor had disassembled the desk lamp and was now carefully extracting a vintaric crystal lightbulb.

'Yes, I spoke to Mya. She's also reassigned two of the bar staff to man the security desk.'

Ruby closed her eyes. 'I did catch a glimpse of some plans, but I can't remember, it's so fuzzy. Explosions maybe. Why can't I remember? There's another thing, though. Fala didn't look so good. Sort of feverish, really hot and really sweaty.'

'I've seen that before,' said the Doctor. 'Everything reminds me of something else. It must be connected…'

Just then there was a knock at the door. The Doctor walked over and opened it to find Mya, Lori and Nazari standing on the other side. He invited them into the room. 'Brilliant timing! We were just discussing a plan. This is one of those situations where a plan would come in handy. Don't you think?'

Nazari and Mya didn't respond, just nodded awkwardly in vague agreement. They stood at opposite ends of the room, visibly avoiding eye contact.

Ruby giggled to herself. She could recognise this scenario a mile off, even without the assistance of a telepathic crystal planet. She was right back in secondary school, reliving her teenage years, knee-deep in the middle of the unbearable love triangle/third wheel combo. The way Lori had just smiled and bounced into the room, she figured he was blissfully unaware of the unspoken tension between Mya and Nazari. Typical man.

'Such a hectic day, but it's *awfully* nice to have everyone banded together.' Lori smiled blissfully.

After some polite, non-committal smiles, eventually Mya spoke. 'Doctor, I called a full staff meeting, and nobody has seen Fala. Ruby, did she tell you where she was going?'

'Nah, and I really didn't get a good look at the guy who let us in. The corridors were so dim, and he wore a mask. But I do know she is hell-bent on making sure this ceremony doesn't go ahead.'

'I propose we call off the Ijoa for everyone's safety,' Mya said confidently. For the first time since they'd entered the suite, Nazari looked at her. The shock, scrawled across her face, told a story of betrayal.

'Mya, we can't,' Nazari responded fiercely.

Mya found a blank spot on a wall and didn't take her eyes off it. 'I know, I know how important the Ijoa is. But it's too dangerous, we can't risk any more casualties. Two dead bodies on Kubuntu's sacred ground. Two! The Gardens are suffering. Kubuntu's teachings are adamant that the dead and the living remain separate. I won't risk any more. Not you, not my staff, no one.'

Her gaze finally met Nazari's piercing blue eyes.

Lori put a shy finger up as a form of polite interjection. 'If I could just ... Obviously, I'm more than happy to defer to the majority. That being said, I don't particularly want to be the one to put more people in danger. Equally, I'd also rather not bring shame to my family name, so I really am torn. What do you think, Doctor?' Lori took a deep breath.

'Well—' began the Doctor.

Before he could exhale, Lori started up again. 'I also don't want it said that the Prince of Bia was seen to be negotiating with terrorists. And being the first of my bloodline to both restart and then break again hundreds of thousands of years of tradition on top of that does not a good leader make. The people of Bia will rebel. That's all we need.' At this stage, Lori was practically hyperventilating. 'Ooh, this is new, I have never forgotten how to breathe before.'

Ruby sprang up and ushered him over to the bed, where she guided his head between his legs and rubbed his back. 'Thank *gasp* you *gasp* Ruby *gasp* Sunday *gasp*,' Lori managed, his head still between his legs.

'The Ijoa must go ahead tomorrow as planned. There are people – *my* people – who depend on it, who depend on the Gardens,' Nazari said defiantly. 'There will be no question of "if", only "how" – is that understood?'

'What a woman,' Ruby said in full admiration, as Mya suppressed a smile.

The Doctor stood silent for a while. Eventually, he said, 'I can't protect you both. Those Bia who attacked are still out there and if I can't figure out how they got in, I can't stop it happening again even with the locked telepads. And then there's Fala, who is heaven knows where, planning who knows what.' He began pacing again. 'She also clearly has staff on the inside protecting her. There are too many loose ends, too many variables, and you lot, as brilliant as you are, have no structures in place to keep any of you safe.'

Nazari's face scrunched up as she weighed up her options. Finally, she smiled. 'You protect Lori and... I will be fine, I'll have Mya.'

'You can also have me,' Ruby said confidently. 'I'll protect you!'

'Nope!' The Doctor jumped up. 'No, no, not a chance, I'm not letting you out of my sight.'

'Doctor, I'll be fine,' said Ruby. 'I promise.'

'I will be there too, Doctor,' Mya said reassuringly.

The Doctor scanned the faces of the women in front of him. They seemed so assured of themselves. 'Fine.' He rummaged in his pocket and pulled out a remote with a single button. 'First sign of danger, you press this. It will signal the sonic and relay it down to me on this screen.' He held out the remote to Ruby.

Ruby took it and saluted. 'Aye-aye, captain.'

'Okay, so what is the next phase of the Ijoa?' the Doctor asked.

'Nazari will enter the sanctuary to seek approval and guidance from her ancestors, the descendants of Kubuntu,' said Mya.

Lori leapt to his feet, having quickly recovered from his minor panic attack. 'And I will commune with the High Council of Bia in the sacred baths to do the same.' He stopped, a wave of sadness washing over his face. He hung his head. 'I suppose I also must replace... *appoint* a new adviser.' After a moment of pensive silence, he continued, 'Oh, Doctor, maybe you could... I don't exactly have the capacity to do interviews right now. There's no time. As well as keeping me safe, a man as ancient as you must have the best advice.'

'But I'm not Bia...'

'That won't be an issue. I will walk you through it.' He continued flippantly, 'There's a bath... in milk and honey... at night. You'll be fine, you can swim, right? Will you? Please...' Lori clasped his hands together and pouted. 'Please Doctor, don't make me do the eyes too.' He continued to put on some of the cutest puppy dog eyes the Doctor had ever seen.

'Okay, fine,' the Doctor conceded, rolling his eyes.

'Yessss! Brilliant!' Overjoyed, Lori bounced over to him and put a long arm around his shoulders. A chill travelled down the Doctor's spine and continued through the nerve endings in his back. It felt like a cold shower on a hot day, and it comforted him deeply. He found his stress melting away.

Mya walked over to the door and opened it up. 'I'm putting the place on lockdown. I'm sending non-essential guests and staff home. The Bia High Court and their guests are welcome to remain, but that is it. Only guests of the Ijoa.' She turned to Lori; he still had the Doctor secured firmly under his arm.

'Hmm? Yes. I will get a message out to the expected guests right away. No plus-ones.' He put two thumbs up.

Mya rolled her eyes. 'What does that mean?'

'I'm not sure. I saw Ruby do it, and I thought it looked cool.' Lori looked around for Ruby's approval.

'Very cool!' Ruby laughed, shooting a double thumbs-up right back at him.

'See. Very cool!'

Mya rolled her eyes again. She looked each of them in the eye as she continued. 'Everyone must stay vigilant. The ceremonies will start in one hour, before the sun falls.' She opened the door and marched away.

'What a spirited woman!' Lori said. 'I think I might be in love,' he added with a smile.

Nazari's own smile faded in an instant, as did her tattoos. The Doctor and Ruby exchanged an awkward glance, but both decided to keep their noses out of it.

'I must prepare,' Nazari said as she made her way to the door. 'I will see you all later.'

Lori lifted his arm off the Doctor and skipped over to the exit. 'Me too. Doctor, I will see you later. I'll have the ceremonial robes prepared for you. This is exciting.'

Ruby and the Doctor found themselves alone again in their hotel room.

'Mya and Nazari ... they're, like, a thing, right?'

The Doctor opened his mouth, primed with all the gossip, and then stopped. He had an idea. 'All the guests and staff members have their DNA scanned into the biometric systems. Mya and Fala are twins ...'

'So if you scanned for them against the resort's live database, there would be two almost identical DNA signatures that would appear,' Ruby finished.

'Exactly.'

'I've got this space detective thing down to an art. Dunno why you make it look so intense sometimes,' Ruby said casually as she climbed back onto the bed, searching for her next snack.

'Oi, sassy, cool it, yeah. I did most of the legwork. You basically just finished an alley-oop.'

'So how do we get Mya's DNA?'

The Doctor frowned. 'I thought you didn't want to hear my very clever explanations because you were on holiday.'

Ruby laughed. 'Go on, I know you're dying to!'

The Doctor smiled; he loved a monologue.

With the crystal lightbulb in one hand, the Doctor skipped over to the hotel room monitor. 'If this thing can call the front desk and display a map of the Gardens, then I should be able to create a security relay between the systems and the sonic without having to bypass the biometric deadlock.' He disconnected the front-facing panel, exposing the internal wiring. He plugged the sonic into an exposed port and then connected it to a tiny screen he pulled out of his clutch. 'Only issue is that the sonic has to stay in the room or the signal won't be strong enough. But with a few tweaks this should manage basic sonic functions.' He made the last few minute adjustments and then presented it to Ruby. 'Now this will beep and light the bulb every time the security system is triggered.'

Ruby tapped her temple with her finger. 'Very clever.'

The Doctor curtseyed. 'Thank you. Thank you very much.'

About half an hour later, after much tinkering and fiddling, the Doctor climbed into bed next to Ruby, who had recently found the hot massage setting on the mattress.

'Very nice,' he said, allowing the warm vibrations to work their magic over his body. He then pointed at the monitor of a makeshift security relay device, cobbled together from hotel room parts. In the middle of the floorplan displayed on the screen were two blinking dots. 'That's us.'

Ruby waved at the manifestation of herself. The Doctor scrolled down multiple floors to find Mya's blinking dot on the foyer. 'Now if I isolate her DNA signature, I should be able to—' The Doctor stopped in his tracks. He scrolled up and down two or three times. 'There's no other signature that matches Mya's.'

'Do twins not work the same here?'

'Even if they were fraternal twins, there would be a 50 per cent match... somewhere.' The Doctor looked up at Ruby. 'Either Fala isn't in the Gardens or she isn't really Mya's twin.'

Ruby's eyes widened with intrigue.

KNOCK! KNOCK! KNOCK!

The Doctor rolled out of bed and walked over to the door to find Lori, beaming as always, holding an elegantly finished gift box across both arms.

'It's time, Doctor.'

Nine

Minutes later, the Doctor found himself in a changing room in the basement of the resort.

'What do you think?' Lori asked him nervously. He had been silently staring at himself in the mirror for quite some time now. 'I know they're a little... big. Bia Can was a lot... wider than you.' He smiled, apparently proud of himself for his excellent inoffensive phrasing.

The Doctor looked down at the ceremonial robes draped over his body. 'They're beautiful. The blend of organic fabric and advanced empathetic crystalline technology is...' It didn't happen very often, almost never, but the Doctor found himself lost for words.

'The fabric itself is as old as the first Ijoa – passed down for generations. The Bia, however, are born ready with industry and evolution in their bones, so they naturally began to devise ways of incorporating technology into the robes.'

The Doctor ran his fingers along the material; the soft silky texture glided underneath his palms so smoothly that his hand felt weightless. All over the robe were embroidered runes stitched from bioluminescent fibres that glowed as he touched them.

Lori continued. 'Over time, as the Bia evolved, they lost touch with their inner selves. Yewa are taught to engage meaningfully with their emotions from birth. So as a people they grew to wear their hearts on their sleeve.'

'The tattoos!'

Lori nodded. 'The Bia eventually engineered their robes to reflect the same, as a reminder that they are more than their industry or productivity.'

The Doctor watched as the embroidery shone brighter in response to his fascination. Slowly, the intricate patterns and symbols began to rearrange themselves and move across the plane of the cloth.

Lori kept talking as he adjusted the Doctor's now lopsided robe. 'Each rune represents a key aspect of the wearer's culture, their history, their philosophy, even their cosmic connections.'

The Doctor wondered to himself what these symbols would become; he'd had so many faces, been so many people. A healer, a traveller, a warrior. What would his clothes reveal about who he was now? The symbols belonging to Bia Can slowly dissipated. The Doctor held his breath. So much of who he knew he was now mystified him. He watched with anticipatory silence as new stitches formed in the fabric: the unique calligraphy of High Gallifreyan. He smiled sadly, running his fingers once again over the elegant loops and curves of his mother tongue. 'Nano-scale circuitry woven into ancient fabric, creating a dynamic display that pulsates in tandem with the wearer's emotional and physical energy... Honestly, the Bia are brilliant. Genius!'

Lori bounded closer to the Doctor, grabbed him by the shoulders and turned him round to face him. 'Ooh, you haven't even seen the best part. Close your eyes and focus on just being present. Who are you right now, in this second?'

As Lori slowly backed away, the Doctor did as he asked. He closed his eyes and concentrated on who he was now. He let his past selves fade momentarily to the back of his mind and simply existed.

'Now open.'

The Doctor lifted his eyelids to find the circuits in his robe now projected holographic images of High Gallifreyan in the air around him. The Doctor had spent so much time absorbing other cultures from all over the universe, he rarely found himself immersed in his own.

'It's rare to think about home in such a state of peace,' he said contentedly.

Lori smiled. 'Come, Doctor, we must head to the baths.'

The Doctor nodded and, as he turned to follow him, the projections disappeared.

Side by side, the Doctor and Lori walked through a set of great double doors and into the spa's reception area.

Like the rest of Yewa's greatest wonder, the reception of the spa was a blend of nature and advanced technology powered by various crystals. The plants, however, seemed sad. Like they hadn't given up yet but were well on their way to ruin.

A dormant Light Wraith stood behind the front desk. The Doctor eyed it warily.

As he and Lori crossed the long steamy foyer to the baths, the ambient light of Yewa's moon reflected off the purple amethyst and sugilite adorning the walls of the room, creating a slow disco effect.

Lori raised his eyebrows. 'Romantic, isn't it?' He smiled blissfully. The room was so still, so tranquil, even the signature mist around the Wraith barely moved. Although he wasn't aware of any actual ailments in his body, the moment the Doctor set his bare foot on the mosaic crystal floor, he felt himself healing. He felt stronger, taller, sharper, like someone had flicked an 'on' switch in the atoms that made up his cells. The noise that had been swimming around his head completely shut off. Then, something shifted. A whisper.

Danger, get out, get out now, wake up, it is near.

'You all right, Doctor?'

'Did you hear that?' He turned around quickly, as if to catch out the Wraith behind him. 'Go ahead, I'll join you in a minute,' he said to Lori, who had positioned himself in between another set of doors.

Lori flashed him another confident thumbs-up; he'd really got into them. The Doctor waited for him to disappear into the baths before turning to face the Wraith.

'What are you? What are you really?' he demanded as he crept closer to the creature. Maybe it was toying with him, playing a game of hide and seek, lying dormant waiting for the perfect time to darken its shroud.

The Doctor crept closer and closer. The mist around the Wraith had gained some energy, but the creature itself remained perfectly still. 'I can't figure you out. You're so familiar. I've seen you before but I keep forgetting.'

Suddenly, the Wraith turned its head to meet the Doctor's gaze. The Doctor tried to take a step back but found himself rooted to the ground. He couldn't move. The white void that stood in place of a face began to leak out of the creature's hood and encased its host until it was just pure mist. The white mist rushed towards the Doctor. He willed himself to move, but his body just didn't comply. With the power and speed of a freight train, the mist attacked directly at the Doctor's torso and passed through the other side before dissipating into thin air.

Short of breath, the Doctor began wheezing. He fell to his knees, gasping for air, his chest tightening. One heart had given way completely and the other was ready to follow. As the respiratory distress overwhelmed him, his knees too gave way and he was now flat on the floor. He could hear warnings and appeals echoing around his brain.

The Empire is near. Save us, Doctor. The Empire is near. Save our daughters.

He attempted a final gasp for air and rolled onto his back. Out of the corner of his eye, he saw an alcove with a quaint water feature. He channelled all remaining energy into his arms, dragging himself across the floor to position himself in the water feature. He opened his mouth and let the healing waters of the Ratehs river work their magic. His silent heart began to bump in unison with the other and then ... he was fine. Completely fine, as if nothing bad had happened, ever.

'I hate anti-climaxes,' he said as he shot to his feet. He looked around for the Wraith, but it was nowhere to be seen. 'I can still feel you. You're still here. You want my attention? You have it! I'm listening, I want to help. What is the Empire?'

No answer.

'So what was that, a wakeup call?' It dawned on the Doctor. 'Aah no, not a wakeup call, a call to action!' The guardians of the Garden were crying out, but yet again he could feel his sense of urgency slipping. *I must remember to care*, he thought repeatedly. He made it his mantra.

'Let's get this show on the road. The Ijoa will mean answers, answers will mean solutions.' He looked to the place where the Wraith once sat and made a promise: 'Solutions will mean action.' The Bia had their own time to commune with the ancestors. He'd talk to those ancestors himself and see what he could figure out.

As the Doctor crossed the threshold into the hot baths, he was swaddled by a comforting wave of warmth and the intoxicating aroma of fragranced oils and aromatic perfumes. Lori, perched on a stone, looked over and smiled.

'Baths is a bit of a misnomer, isn't it?' the Doctor said as he stared down at a single, 25-metre swimming pool that had been hand-carved from the crystalline rock formations.

Lori chuckled. 'I guess you're right.' He hadn't been exaggerating. The bath was literally filled with warm milky water and the Doctor could smell the sweet honey. 'Where have you been?'

The Doctor thought for a moment. He couldn't quite recall what had happened in the last two minutes and didn't much care either. 'Exploring,' he said, now suddenly cautious, keeping his cards to his chest.

He analysed the ancient runes and intricate mosaics that adorned the walls, each depicting hieroglyphic folk tales of the history between Bia and Yewa. Most of it had chipped or fallen away, so he struggled to piece together a single full story. He paused in front of a vase-sized marble statue in an alcove near the steps down into the bath. It was Kubuntu, although in perfect condition. There were was an indent in her chest, the size of a large jewel, with delicate carvings around its edge, suggesting it had once held something precious.

The Doctor turned to find Lori, soaking in the far corner of the bath, waving him over. He walked around the edge and placed the robe on a hook next to Lori's.

He then pulled out his makeshift security relay from an inside pocket and checked the monitor for the whereabouts of all the key players. Fala was still nowhere to be seen; Ruby, Mya and Nazari were all in the inner sanctum. He placed the monitor on the floor behind Lori as he stepped into the pool and let the water wash over his body. 'Oof! Geothermal systems, ensuring the perfect balance of temperature in relation to the skin. The genius, it just doesn't stop.'

Shimmers in the milky water rippled past him. He looked down at his feet to find luminescent mosses and algae peeping through the cracks in the crystal mosaic and emitting a gentle soothing glow. The Doctor felt stronger than ever, like he could have singlehandedly built the pyramids of ancient Egypt. With one hand.

'I know that smile.' Lori pointed a playful finger at the Doctor's beaming face. 'One of our biggest trades. The healing waters are sourced from the deep underground reservoirs of the River Ratehs. They contain enriched minerals that formed over a billion years and can only be found on Yewa.'

'Not on Bia?' the Doctor asked.

Lori shook his head. 'You feel strong, don't you? I bet you're never going to want to leave,' he laughed.

The Doctor laughed too; Lori was right. He didn't want to leave. He could stay here forever.

'Speaking of never leaving,' Lori continued gleefully. 'There is the man of the hour.' He made a deliberate attempt to sober his tone out of respect. 'How are you keeping, my friend?'

The Doctor turned to see Bia Toh skulking in through the entrance.

'Poor man, he must be a shell of himself,' Lori whispered to the Doctor, indicating Bia Toh's robe. From a distance, it looked completely blank. The circuits in the stitches were so dim, they blended into the rest of the robe. 'Come, Bia Toh, let the waters restore you.'

Bia Toh stopped and bowed weakly. As he took his first steps into the still, warm waters and waded over to Lori and the Doctor, he began to smile. By the time he had arrived in their little corner, he was back to his old cantankerous self. 'Just what I needed,' he sighed as he settled into the water.

After him, three other Bia men entered, disrobed and joined them in the baths. 'These men are also from the High Court. They've been here even longer than Bia Toh,' Lori informed the Doctor. 'Bia Chey, Bia Tatu and Bia Ugon, meet the Doctor.'

'Pleasure. So what now?' the Doctor asked, eager to get the ceremony under way. Now, in the presence of others, he didn't feel quite himself and figured the quicker it started and ended, the faster he could get back to whatever he was meant to be doing. Which was what? *Think, Doctor, think.*

'Well… this,' Lori said casually, interrupting the Doctor's train of thought.

'What?'

'This. We do this. Relax, pamper, have a gab, have a gossip, you know, men stuff,' Lori replied.

'Men stuff…' The Doctor was perplexed. 'So, there's no seeking counsel from the ancestors?'

The men of the Bia High Court laughed raucously.

Bia Toh sighed. 'Ah, thank you, Doctor, I really needed that. No, we won't be engaging in such avid displays of superstition. All that communing with the ancestors, well, it's just folklore. We just say we do to keep the tradition alive but no, it's not really our thing. We commune with the living.'

The Doctor rose to his feet. 'So why do you need me here, then? There are a million other things I could be doing, like—'

'Like what?' Lori asked. 'Your friend is safe, Nazari is safe, we are safe. What is there left for you to do, Doctor?'

'I have to figure out how they got in and why—'

'Why what? Who cares about the why or the how? The only thing that matters is the now. And for now, we are all fine.'

'How can you not care that there are attackers on the loose? Bia Can and the Bia vigi…' The Doctor lost wind as he looked around at Lori and the court. They shrugged apathetically.

'I guess it will have to be a bridge we cross once we reach it,' said Lori. 'For now, relax, Doctor, you're meant to be on holiday. And as my temporary vizier, your one job is to sit and gossip.' He tugged on the Doctor's arm, forcing him to sit back down. 'You need to relax,' he said emphatically.

'That reminds me, sire,' a voice said, cutting through the tension. It was Bia Chey. 'Your Highness, have you thought of a replacement for the vizier position?'

It was now Bia Toh's turn to jump to his feet. Outraged, he shouted, 'How dare you? How dare you, Bia Chey? Bia Can's crystals have not even touched the ground.'

Bia Chey held his hand up in apology. 'I understand, Bia Toh. But we must think of our future. There are trade partners from all over Chimandra coming tomorrow. We must think of Bia.'

'Bia is fine,' Bia Toh scoffed. 'Tell me, in the years we've been here, when last did you receive a prayer?' Silence fell over the room as he waited for a response. 'Exactly.'

'Well, it's not up to you, is it, Bia Toh?' Bia Chey got to his feet and walked towards Lori, making sure to deliberately brush past Bia Toh for good measure. 'Your Highness?'

Bia Toh turned and attempted to grab Bia Chey.

'Patience, Bia Toh, patience,' Lori said, restraining him gently by the arm. He smiled. 'So, Bia Chey, you want to be my vizier. What makes you better than Bia Ugon or Bia Tatu here?'

Bia Chey scoffed at the comparison.

'And what is that supposed to mean?' asked Bia Ugon indignantly. He was a slender man, but animated. When he spoke, he made sure to engage all his appendages in order to fully embody the emotion of whatever he was conveying. Bia Tatu, by contrast, was the strong, silent type. By far the tallest and most chiselled of the men in the bath, he sat very still, as if in a constant meditative state, refusing to exert any more energy than was strictly necessary.

'You know what it means,' Bia Chey spat. 'I have a hundred years of experience on you both combined. Tatu is only here because he inherited his position. He has no real leadership qualities.'

Suddenly, Bia Tatu lunged at Chey. The water activated as tensions passed simmering point, and the milky liquid began to boil over the sides of the pool, crashing onto the tiles. The Doctor could feel the energy of past grievances and bruised egos stoking the bath, increasing the temperature. The entire pool was now effectively a massive jacuzzi.

He sat up, prepared to leap to safety should the temperature rise any further. *The stupidity and ineptitude of patriarchy will prevail in all galaxies,* he thought to himself. After several failed attempts to quell the clash of egos, coupled with obscene gestures and ostentatious grandstanding which caused the crystals to flicker erratically, the Doctor – who traditionally had no time for such obvious displays of peacocking – found himself on high alert. *Distance your mind.* The water had lulled his body into a false sense of security, but something in the atmosphere had shifted. He grew increasingly fixated on the events unfolding in front of him. He could taste the torrent of emotions that had built up between the men. It tasted like old pears. That was the worst part.

A sudden storm had erupted over the bath, and a white fog hovered over the once tranquil waters.

The first blow came from Bia Tatu. It was swift and unexpected, landing square across Bia Chey's cheek. Then a wild swing sliced through the air at emphatic speed and planted itself in Bia Ugon's gut, sending him flying across the breadth of the pool. He landed with a resounding splash, sending shockwaves rippling through the water. In the chaos that ensued, bodies collided and thrashed, each man grappling for dominance in the shallow water. All of a sudden, the water picked up speed and began swirling, with Lori and the Doctor as the centre of the ensuing whirlpool.

'The ego of men, eh?' Lori laughed. 'I don't know why you're doing all this fighting; the Doctor is the one who currently has the job.'

Before he could respond, the Doctor found himself whisked up into the vortex, round and round with the rest of the High Court.

As he inhaled involuntary gulps of the pool, Lori widened his stance, prepping himself for the moment the Doctor would pass him again. He rocked back and forth, looking for the perfect time to reach out and grab the Doctor, pulling him into the safety of the eye of the storm. The water that churned around them, frothing and swirling, stopped in an instant as the men stopped fighting momentarily.

One by one, they released each other from their clenched fists and forceful grasps and turned to the Doctor. They slowly waded towards him, with menace in their eyes.

'Bia Toh… what are you doing? Stop this at once,' ordered Lori. 'Bia Chey? Bia Tatu? Bia Ugon? What is the meaning of this?' He stood in front of the Doctor.

The men continued to make for the Doctor, the 'vizier' that stood in their way, as if possessed by angry jealousy, their eyes all dark as night.

Lori stepped aside to face the Doctor. 'Should we?' With a nod of his head, he indicated the door on the other side of the pool.

'Yep, yep, yep,' the Doctor agreed.

The two men clambered out of the pool and put on their robes. Bia Chey, Bia Ugon, Bia Tatu and Bia Toh, still focused on the Doctor, continued to wade towards them.

BANG! BANG! BANG!

The men turned to find the source of the banging.

Fala and the Firebrand had burst through the double doors and, with military precision, surrounded the pool. The Doctor's eyes darted left to right as he took in the situation. Lori by his side, the Bia High Court in the pool, five Firebrand members across each length and Fala standing directly opposite them. He was used to being outnumbered, but usually they all had the same agenda. He could use this to his advantage, maybe?

The Doctor looked around. The security relay had been washed away in the chaos, swept against a wall. He rushed over and picked it up. The screens were blank: not a single alarm, no signs of a breach.

'By order of the Firebrand—' Fala began.

'Wait!' the Doctor yelled. 'I just need a bit of quiet for a sec.'

His brazen swagger stunned all present silent. Here was a man facing multiple threats, an angry Bia High Court and armed Firebrand insurgents, and *he* was telling *them* to wait. The Court started their fuss again and were immediately met with, 'I told you to wait. You want to kill me, they want to kill you, everybody will get their chance in a second, but I need a moment.' He scrolled through the floor plans, from the top floor all the way to the basement.

Fala was standing right in front of him. There she was, as large as life, but her little blinking dot was nowhere to be found on the screen in his hand. 'It just doesn't make sense... Unless...'

Fala cocked her gun. The rest of the Firebrand followed suit.

'Doctor, I think we are now at that bridge,' Lori said playfully.

'Lori, Prince of Bia, you will order your people to leave this place at once,' Fala said.

'Never thought I'd go out in my swim trunks.' He smiled back.

'Is this really the time for cute banter?' the Doctor asked, thoroughly stressed with Lori's response to immediate danger.

'You and your men are ordered to leave, or these waters will run red with your blood,' Fala hissed.

The Doctor stepped in front of Lori, and the Firebrand turned their guns away from the Bia High Court and pointed them at him. 'Whoa, whoa, whoa. What is the meaning of all this? Cold-blooded murder cannot be the answer, Fala,' the Doctor said. 'Please. Or ... is it Fala?'

Fala was momentarily taken aback. Something about her face changed. Not her expression as such, but for a moment, a split second, the Doctor saw her face transform into someone else's.

'You should have left already. I warned Ruby.' Fala turned her attention to one of the Firebrand members. 'Dana, Kill him.'

The young woman looked up at Fala, her eyes awash with shock.

'You heard me, Dana,' insisted Fala. 'Kill the Doctor.'

Following instructions, Dana looked at the Doctor apologetically and raised her weapon.

'Where's Fala? The real Fala? You can't be her, unless ...'

'Why are you doing this?' Bia Chey demanded. 'We have made a home here. This planet is as much ours as it is yours – terrorists.'

'Us? Terrorists?' Dana smiled. 'At every Ijoa the Bia come and—'

Bia Chey jumped out of the pool with ungodly agility and lunged at her. He grabbed the weapon and turned it against her, backing towards Lori and the Doctor with Dana in a headlock. He released her but kept the nozzle firmly pressed against her back.

'Fala, I'm scared,' Dana said.

Fala simply shrugged. The Doctor watched as the girl's eyes filled with tears at the shock of the betrayal.

Bia Chey powered down the safety.

'No!' the Doctor cried.

Too late. Bia Chey shot Dana in the back and the young woman's body turned instantly to crystal.

The Doctor's mouth dropped open in shock. He lunged at Bia Chey and grabbed the weapon with one hand, then threw it into the pool. 'One more move and I blow us all up,' he said holding up the security relay device as if it was a detonator.

'You're bluffing,' said Fala.

'I am most definitely not,' said the Doctor. He most definitely was, but he couldn't let them know that. 'If there is one thing you should know about me, there are several things you should know about me. One, I don't like guns, never have, never will. Two, I hate being threatened – I just find it extremely rude, if I'm honest. Three, I will do anything to protect my friends, anything. Now I want you to look into my eyes because I may have been many people but I'm told my eyes don't change much. I have more blood on my hands than you can know. And I will not let a drop of yours bother my conscience if it means protecting my friend. No one lives, everyone dies. That's what we all want, clearly, isn't it? Carnage? Hellfire? I've wired this security relay to the Garden's irrigation systems. I push this button and we are all going down. One more move, I blow this whole joint to the ground.'

A few of the Firebrand lowered their weapons.

Fala shook her head. 'He's bluffing. He said it himself – he would never endanger his precious Ruby. Take aim.'

The Firebrand rearmed themselves but, without clarity of instruction, they all pointed their guns in different directions, some at Lori and the Doctor, others at the Bia High Court.

'All right, then. Plan two!' The Doctor pressed a button on the security relay.

A wailing alarm immediately blared over the room, an agonising screech. The Firebrand dropped their weapons to clutch their ears. Bia Ugon was the first of the Bia High Court to take advantage of the disruption. He clambered over the others in an attempt to climb out of the pool. Bia Tatu and Bia Toh were not far behind him.

Lori grabbed the Doctor by the hand and yanked him towards a plain wall behind them. He waved it open and pulled him through, leaving it open just long enough for the rest of the Court to get through as they dodged and weaved to avoid the heavy fire of Fala's tiny army.

'I'm sorry, Doctor,' Bia Toh said. 'Sorry I attacked you; I don't know what came over me.'

'No time.' The Doctor tapped away at the screen. Outside he could hear the Firebrand regrouping, banging at the walls. 'Right, they should be deadlocked in there for now but...'

'But what?'

Grimly, the Doctor turned the screen around to show the men in front of him how several black blinking dots were converging on one place. 'The alarms are summoning the Wraiths to the inner sanctum.'

'I know a shortcut,' Bia Chey said, leading the charge down the corridor.

Ten

Once again completely oblivious to the impending doom that was fast approaching her location, an awestruck Ruby stood at the intersection of paths in the middle of the inner sanctum.

The air in the temple around her carried the faint scent of exotic flowers not dissimilar to the ones she had encountered when they first arrived. But this time, there was a discernible difference: these blooms smelt more naturally sweet, whereas in the market there'd been a manufactured tang sitting beneath the aroma. Like the difference between fresh strawberries and a strawberry-flavoured sweet. She looked down at the temple's labyrinth of intricately carved paths, each lined with various iridescent flora, which led to either an exit, another path or a small altar.

I call on Kubuntu for guidance.

Ruby spun to find the source of the ghoulish whisper she had just heard.

I call on my ancestors for insight.

Another voice, this time from behind her. She spun again.

Replace my eyes with yours so I may see truth.

The countless voices climbed on top of and crashed into each other. She could feel the weight of history squeezing her from every direction. Millions of souls whispering the remnants of ancient rituals and echoes of forgotten prayers.

When her initial panic cleared, Ruby found the pressure against her body felt less like squeezing and more like holding. She felt held, as if the disembodied voices were the only thing keeping her upright.

She felt weightless.

Ruby looked down at her feet to check if they were still on the ground. They were, but barely; you could just about slide a single sheet of paper between the soles of her feet and the path under them. Ruby smiled. The peace she had felt when she first landed on Yewa had returned and made her feel invincible.

'Honestly, it just doesn't stop,' she marvelled to herself, looking around at the pristine condition of the ancient temple. Usually when something had been abandoned for thousands of years, it turned to ruins, but time didn't have the same effect on Yewa as it did on Earth.

She found herself drawn to a particular flower. The prismatic petals provided an ever-shifting display of hues which reflected in the crystal-clear droplets that trickled into the myriads of water features, streams and ponds throughout the sanctum.

Achoo. The flower expelled tiny pools of light pollen from its stamen, and it sneezed again.

'Bless you,' she said. 'A flower that's allergic to itself, absolute nightmare.' She suddenly realised that she had been dillydallying and there were people waiting for her. 'Okay, what did Mya say to do when I arrived?' She stood for a moment wondering why anyone thought it was a good idea to let her loose on her own in their most holy sanctum.

'Ruby, is that you?' a voice said. 'Follow the brook.' It was Mya; Ruby remembered the sound of her voice.

'Yeah, it's me, just coming through now.' She turned 90 degrees and followed the stream of babbling water, through a gentle rustle of large leaves, until she found herself standing at the foot of a towering statue of Kubuntu.

Carved from onyx black marble and accented with four jewels and precious stones, Kubuntu held in her outstretched hands a glowing orb of bright white light.

Up until this moment, Ruby hadn't yet seen any real depictions of Kubuntu, only the player in the market and the dilapidated hieroglyphics in the catacombs.

She was beautiful. The kind of beauty that makes you re-evaluate the very meaning of the word.

Ruby took a single step forward but, before her foot could contact the ground, she found herself being tugged towards the base of the statue. She began to panic, kicking and boxing the air.

Being caught in a tractor beam was traditionally not a fun experience for her.

But she took solace in the smiles of Mya and Nazari, who were waiting on the other side.

She allowed herself to relax.

Back in the tunnels, the Doctor's legs began to feel heavy. It wasn't an unusual experience for him – simultaneously running towards and away from danger – but this level of mental and physical exhaustion felt foreign. Led by Bia Chey, he sprinted through the erratic network of tunnels with Lori and the two other members of the court. With every twist and turn, the corridors seemed to grow narrower, compressing the very breath from his lungs.

Lori stopped, drenched in sweat. 'Go on without me,' he wheezed.

'No, we're not leaving you,' Bia Toh said, doubling back to check on his prince.

'We really don't have time for this,' the Doctor replied, trying to strike a balance between supportive and insistent. He looked down at his monitor screen. 'The Wraiths are …' He trailed off.

'What, Doctor?' Lori asked.

The Doctor blinked, then smacked the side of the device. It had begun glitching. Static lines appeared and disappeared on the screen like rewound VHS footage. He smacked it again and the image restored.

'Much more effective than a sonic,' he said. 'Right, the Wraiths are still moving to the inner sanctum.' He stopped again, scrolling through the map of the tunnels before him. 'We haven't got any closer. We've been going round in circles.' He turned to Bia Chey and sniffed the air. 'Thermal charges.'

Suddenly the sound of pursuant footsteps echoed through the tunnels.

'Fala,' Bia Toh said fearfully.

'We need to move,' the Doctor said, abandoning the notion of support and leaning fully into insistent.

Bia Chey took off again, and the others followed. This time, however, the Doctor upped his pace and moved forward as leader of the pack, relying on the screen for navigation. He felt himself having to try extra hard to concentrate; there were whispers coming from the walls.

Be alert...

He attempted to block the whispers out, but he couldn't help feeling that they were important. What could they mean? The Gardens needed something...? He put a pin in that train of thought. The sound of drum-like footsteps and fury-filled chanting was drawing nearer. They continued running, through twisting and turning, dimly lit passageways and long shadowy corridors.

'We're going left at the T-junction,' the Doctor yelled without looking back. Something about the whispers was still bothering him. Ever since the spa, there'd been these echoes of voices in his head, but they all spoke at once, so all he could manage was a word here and a phrase there. What empire? The Bia Empire, was that the ancestors' issue?

The Shadows. Watch the shadows.

And there were the voices again. The shadows were now dancing, the same choreography from the festival in the market. What was casting the shadows?

He turned left and found himself leading the charge into a faction of angry Firebrand members.

'Doctor, you are so stupid,' he said, smacking his palm against his head. 'About face!' he yelled, pivoting 180 degrees. He took the group back the way they had come, down the long, shadowy corridor.

'Doctor,' Bia Ugon said, pointing at a second small armed faction of the Firebrand who had clocked them and were coming their way. The two groups were converging on them.

'Let's take our chances with the impossible shadows,' the Doctor said. He strode off along their only route of escape, with the others close behind but struggling to keep up.

Suddenly, the shadows leapt off the walls and turned into a black mist. The gaseous forms solidified into one massive Wraith, which was gaining on them. Bia Ugon tripped and instantly became a pile of crystal.

There was no time to stop. They had to keep running. Bia Chey began to look worse for wear, sweating and heaving. Without comment or notice, he stopped and turned, facing the Wraith with his arms open – an act of surrender. And, as a bony finger stretched out to touch him, Bia Chey died in front of them. He did not, though, transform into crystals as the others all had; instead, he dissolved into a black mist and was absorbed by the Wraith.

There was no time to mourn. Ruby was in danger, and that was the Doctor's main priority. He started sprinting again, his brain running as fast as his legs. *Three ways to die: collapse in on yourself, turn to crystal and, now, be absorbed. Too many inconsistencies. For this many things to not make sense, it has to be deliberate. Someone or something is deliberately orchestrating this chaos.*

'So what now?' Ruby asked, excited to be a part of the ceremony ahead, even though she had been given little to no detail of what it would entail.

Mya and Nazari knelt facing each other, in a circle of crystals, at the base of the statue. 'Well, now, from what I've read, the Keeper of the Gardens and the heir of Kubuntu join at her altar to ask her for guidance at tomorrow's Ijoa,' Mya said, pointing at the statue.

Nazari smiled and looked up at Ruby, inviting her to join them on the floor. 'And you will bear witness.'

'Ooh, it's like a wedding.' The words fell from Ruby's mouth before she could stop herself. 'I mean, not a wedding, who said anything about weddings?'

Both Mya and Nazari averted their eyes from each other and, in doing so, found themselves staring at Ruby. She turned as red as her name promised, and wished the floor would swallow her whole.

'Oof.' Mya made a face, like she had just eaten an orange after brushing her teeth. 'Ease up on the guilt, Ruby dear, I can taste it from here.' She laughed.

Nazari laughed too, half-fighting back a gag. 'It's very pungent, Ruby.'

'There is no hiding in Kubuntu's sanctum. She will reveal all,' Mya continued with a smile. She tapped the floor next to her, again inviting Ruby to join them.

'Like how much you two mean to each other?' she said, accepting the invitation. 'Every time either of you speak, your tattoos gleam in a way that I haven't seen on Yewa.'

And they did. Mya and Nazari lit up the altar. Now, though, their tattoos flickered with the embarrassment of being called out by this perfect stranger.

'Come on,' added Ruby. 'You can't deny it.'

Mya let herself smile, if only for a moment. 'As much as it kills me to say it, Nazari is right. I know there is no room for both. Once the Ijoa is complete, Nazari and Lori will be joined at the hip. That is the price of our duty, and I am ... fine with that.'

Ruby knew this wasn't true. The hesitation in Mya's voice told her everything.

Mya sighed and continued: 'I wish ... I just wish ...' There was something she needed to say, but she couldn't bring herself to do so.

'What?' asked Nazari, searching for an answer. 'You never talk to me any more. I have been waiting for this moment, a place where even you cannot keep secrets from me. So, what is it, Mya? You wish what? You wish you had never loved me?' She said the last part so flippantly, as if there was no way it could be true. But the silence she was met with revealed all she needed to know. 'Really my lo— Mya?'

Mya blinked back her tears. 'Come, let us start. If we upset ourselves much further, we won't be able to connect with the ancestors.'

'Why?' Ruby asked. 'Also how do you know this stuff? Where are your parents or …?'

She trailed off as she realised that she hadn't seen a single elderly person or even a real adult. No one on the planet could have been more than thirty.

It was now Nazari's turn to blink back her own tears and take a deep breath.

She held up both palms, one to each of the women before her, and wrapped her thumbs around the backs of their hands. 'For the most part, it's instinct… The telepathic fields from the crystals educate us. It takes a lot of emotional and spiritual strength to connect with the ancestors. There must be absolute peace within the descendants and in the sanctum.'

'That's why there's only three of us?'

'To keep the variables low,' Nazari said. One heir, one keeper, one witness. A few hundred years ago, this place would have been full of witnesses, according to the tomes.'

Ruby looked around. The space was so vast that such an intimate gathering felt odd. 'Where are your families?' she asked.

Nazari smiled. 'Family works a little differently here. Yewans are both born and not born; we are reincarnated at birth. We turn to crystal and are returned to the planet. We are in part our ancestors. We can spiritually access their hearts, their minds, their sight. But with every reincarnation without the Ijoa, our connection to the ancestors has grown weaker until now there is nothing. Maybe if we can connect to them again, they can tell us how to save our Gardens.'

As she spoke, the light from Kubuntu's orb lifted from the statue's hands and floated in the midst of them.

'This is the collective consciousness of Kubuntu's descendants – our ancestors. Would you like to meet them too, Ruby?' Nazari asked.

Ruby nodded.

'Hold on tight then,' Nazari instructed. 'Find your peace and hold on to it.'

The light from the orb burst into three different streams and connected each of them at the heart.

Ruby thought of her little flat back in London, of Carla and Cherry. She thought of the Doctor, the TARDIS and their many adventures.

Oops, too far, there were some really stressful moments going on.

Back to the flat. Yes, Mum's cooking, Gran's laughter.

Ruby watched as Nazari's eyes literally changed colour, shape and size. They were her eyes but also not.

'I call on Kubuntu for guidance, I call on my ancestors for insight, replace my eyes with yours so that I may see truth,' Nazari whispered.

Ruby blinked.

When she opened her eyes, she found herself in the pit of a small elliptical amphitheatre, standing in milky-white water surrounded by scores of Yewan ancestors. They spoke in whispers, which echoed sotto voce in a way that skipped past the otic organs and synapses then settled deep into her subconscious. There it was again, that ancient language from the catacombs. A language so old, some words didn't translate into English but, from what Ruby could decipher, the ancestors did not give their blessing and the Ijoa was not to go ahead.

Mya and Nazari exchanged looks. This was their last hope at saving the Gardens and the Yewan race from extinction.

'Why would you say that?' whispered Nazari. 'What do you mean? Our people are dying! Your people are dying.'

There was no response.

Nazari gathered Mya and Ruby to her, crouched over, foreheads touching, a form of mid-match huddle.

'What do we do now?' she asked.

'I'm not sure,' Mya whispered back. 'This is unprecedented.'

'Well, you read the ancient tomes, right?' said Ruby. 'There must be something in there.'

'From what I gathered, the asking for blessing part was mostly ceremonial.' Mya couldn't conceal her rising panic. 'We ask, they say yes, everybody moves on.'

'Only, they're not.' Nazari shook her head. 'Stubbornness runs in your family's veins, clearly.'

'Can't you, I dunno, ask them to clarify?' Ruby asked.

Mya and Nazari spoke and spoke, petitioning the ancestors at length. But no approval was given.

'Our Gardens are under siege, they're dying,' Mya said, her voice growing shrill. 'The Ijoa must go ahead or Yewa is finished!'

Ruby wished the TARDIS could make things clearer for her. Did the translation matrix not work in visions or in whatever was happening here? She could still hear Mya and Nazari as if they were speaking English but—

You wish to understand fully?

Ruby couldn't be sure but felt that the question was directed at her.

History is repeating, and our daughters are stubborn.

Ruby blinked again and found herself transported. She now stood next to Mya and Nazari at the very top of the amphitheatre looking down at where they had just been.

At the beginning of time, when the universe was both vast and nothing, Chimandra was born. A tiny galaxy on the edge of the universe. Chimandra in turn birthed Kubuntu, and Kubuntu was the first life.

Ruby had heard this before; it was the story of how Yewa and Bia came to be. Out of the water, the inner sanctum rose.

And then, many years later, an empire of darkness arose ... and we showed it love ...

Ruby bore witness to brutal scenes in the water below. She, Mya and Nazari watched Ijoa after Ijoa play out in quick succession. Each ended with the Bia ruthlessly decimating the Gardens for harvest and cutting down anyone who got in their way. Mya cried, as women almost identical to her dropped lifelessly to the ground, Keeper after Keeper becoming piles of azure crystal in front of them.

No more. No more.

The ancestors clamoured over each other, the memory too painful to recount. The image began to crumble back into the water. With a dislocating shock, Ruby found herself back in the water. As her senses rallied, she realised Nazari's breathing was growing heavy and laboured.

'What's wrong?' Ruby asked.

'The ancestors' pain is becoming her own. Their connection is too strong.' Mya held Nazari upright, cradling her in her arms as she lowered her to the floor. 'My love, you must stay calm—'

'I have so many questions,' Nazari gasped, clutching her chest. 'But the ancestors ... I can feel it all.'

'You must relax, Nazari, do you hear me? Breathe ...'

And so the cycle repeats.

In that moment, it clicked for Ruby. 'Nazari, you have to stay calm. I know that's the least helpful thing to hear, but that's the reason for the massive secret. That's the reason the Ijoas just stopped happening out of the blue. Learning the truth is so painful, so violent that it's easier to say nothing. Do nothing. Learn nothing. But then you repeat the same mistakes because you never learn. Growth is so painful, because on top of everything else, it messes with the status quo, it's disrupting the peace. Puts the whole "ignorance is bliss" thing in perspective.'

Nazari nodded.

Mya held one hand and put the other on her chest. They drew breath together, regulating each other in tandem until Nazari had calmed down.

'I make peace with the truth, no matter the cost,' Nazari said.

So ... the whole truth?

'Yes, the whole truth, and none of this cryptic roundabout nonsense. Just get to it.' Ruby snapped her fingers, encouraging them to move it along. She wasn't sure where this sense of urgency had come from, but something didn't feel right.

Something felt very wrong.

Ruby looked up at Mya; she could sense it too.

'There's a disturbance in the inner sanctum,' Mya said.

The ancestors were fading, but they exhaled a final message.

Beware the Empire, my daughters.

Beware the Empire.

Ruby suddenly felt herself being ripped from the vision. She fought to concentrate on the peace, hoping that would stabilise her in this world.

But it was too late.

'This way,' the Doctor said as he made another sharp right. 'We're almost there.' *Hang in there, Ruby,* he thought. Up till now, at every turn there had stood either a Wraith or one of Fala's fighters. They had mostly evaded detection, but the Doctor could feel his luck wearing thin.

'Doctor, not sure I can keep this up much longer,' Lori said, leaning on Bia Toh as he ran.

'We're almost there.' The Doctor looked down at his screen and could still see the blinking dots converging on the inner sanctum. 'The Wraiths have gone rogue and are heading straight for Ruby and Nazari.'

They came to a stop, panting for breath, and the Doctor pointed to the wall. 'The inner sanctum is on the other side.' He looked back down at the security relay. There were no longer any blinking dots heading for their location. He stopped for a moment and banged the screen. Nothing changed.

The Doctor took some massive strides back before charging at the door, shoulder first. The door burst open and he found himself in the inner sanctum. Skipping over plants and crystalline rocks, he followed the brook, with Lori and the other two Bia in tow.

'We must be gentle,' said Bia Tatu. 'If Nazari and the others have started their ritual, there must be no disruption to the peace, or it could kill us all.' He rarely spoke, but his face had subtitles and, when he did talk, it was always rational.

'Noted,' the Doctor said as he continued along the brook and through the tall plants. He couldn't reconcile this side of Bia Tatu with the man's random burst of violence earlier. Then the Doctor stopped, hushed his voice. 'The Wraiths are just ahead.' Carefully, he led his party forward until he parted a thicket of undergrowth and came to a sudden, confused halt.

No Wraiths. Only four masked figures pointing weapons at Ruby, Nazari and Mya, who were still in their trance but had begun stirring at the disturbance.

'Don't touch them!' Bia Toh whispered loudly. 'You will break the psionic bond and kill us all.'

At the sound of his voice, one of the figures turned around and dropped his mask.

It was Fran, now without his bellhop uniform, standing before them, as large as life.

'How did you get back in?' the Doctor asked exasperatedly. 'I sent you away. I sent you all away.'

Fran smiled and stepped forward. 'My friends have friends in high places,' he said, pointing at the other three men. With their weapons firmly fixed on Ruby, Mya and Nazari, they turned to look at the Doctor.

They were the Bia vigilantes from the market.

The very same who were also responsible for Bia Can's murder.

'That's not possible.' The Doctor clenched his fists. 'If you touch a hair on Ruby's head—'

'Doctor, I'm fine ... a little headache but I'm fine.' Ruby had woken up from her trance and got warily to her feet, eyeing the weapons all around. 'Ooh. Explains the danger the ancestors were talking about.'

As if on cue, the Doctor heard a voice in his head.

Beware the Empire.

The next moment, Fala and two Firebrand members burst through a side entrance. Also armed, they took position on the other side of Kubuntu's statue.

As the Doctor took stock of his surroundings, and as Lori and the Bia High Court shielded themselves behind him, he felt everything becoming clearer; as if he'd had a blocked nose and now could finally use both nostrils. Something in him switched, an old persona growing dominant for a moment, senses he had tried to deny so many times – the senses of the Doctor of War. They kicked in coolly as he surveyed the combatants at play.

Each group had positioned themselves to form an equilateral triangle. To the Doctor's left, with only a forked brook and a row of waist-high flowers separating them, stood Fala and the Firebrand. Half of them were pointing their weapons at him, while the other half pointed theirs at Fran and the Bia Vigilantes to his right. Fran, across the brook in the centre, was pointing his weapon at the Doctor, with two vigilantes pointing theirs at Fala. The last remaining vigilante and Fala each pointed their weapons at Ruby, Mya and Nazari. The Doctor silently noted the orb that was hovering in front of Nazari, holding her ancestors' spirits.

'Who doesn't love a good old-fashioned standoff?' the Doctor said with a roguish smile. 'Don't you love it? A three-way impasse, tense and precarious. Each party holding a position of equal threat against the others and most brilliantly, no winners. See, this is brilliant, absolutely brilliant. I'm like a Yewan, I'm a reincarnation of myself. I am my own ancestor in many ways. So I can see through old eyes. But seeing and understanding are two different things.'

The Empire is near.

The Doctor stepped forward, and in an instant all weapons were facing him.

'Fala, what are you thinking?' Mya said as calmly as possible. 'Bringing weapons into the inner sanctum! One wrong move and it is the end of Yewa as we know it. Any death in here will damn us all.' She looked down at Nazari, who hadn't budged.

The Doctor could feel the delicate balance of power: any sudden action would trigger a cataclysmic reaction of violence and destruction. The tension in the air was palpable, enhanced by the profusion of crystals that surrounded them. Each person's eyes shifting from left to right as they weighed their options against the potential dire consequences of their actions. 'Well, the good thing is, we're all here. All sides are finally present all in one space. So we can just... talk. No need for violence or destruction, we can all just hear each other out. So who wants to go first?'

A solitary beat passed before each party began screaming and yelling at each other. The white orb in front of Nazari began to pulse and shake, and with that so did Nazari. She convulsed but remained upright. As the yelling continued, the crystals around them began to glow and flicker with increasing speed. Just then two more Firebrands appeared through the leaves and joined Fala.

'EVERYBODY SHUT THE HELL UP!' the Doctor shouted over the mass of voices.

As a sudden silence fell over the room, the light from the orb exploded, flinging Nazari backwards into the statue of Kubuntu.

'Nazari!' Mya cried. She ran to her and held her in her arms.

Making good use of the distraction, Bia Toh and Bia Tatu retraced their steps swiftly, abandoning the Doctor and Lori to fend for themselves. Lori exchanged a glance with Fala before darting off after his subordinates. 'Catch us if you can.'

Following their lead, Fala and her two followers quickly vanished into the inner sanctum. Fran and his masked vigilantes gave chase.

The Doctor leapt over the brook with agility, heading straight for Ruby. He grabbed her hand and hurried her over to Mya and Nazari.

'Is she okay?' he asked, urgency in his voice.

'Unconscious.' Mya sighed with relief, though her worry was evident. 'Her heart is racing.'

The Doctor looked up at the orb. It was pulsating more quickly. There was something about the way it flickered; not on and off, more of a *bum-bum, bum-bum*. Like the beat of a heart. That was it!

'I've got a plan.' The Doctor glanced at his screen, tapping away furiously. 'Well… part of a plan. Well… one-third of a really bad plan. I'm improvising, like jazz.'

'Great, now's as good a time as any,' Ruby said, her tone a mix of sarcasm and hope.

Suddenly, the orb began to shake and pulse erratically.

'Nazari, can you hear me?' Mya called out, panic edging her voice. 'There's something wrong. The connection is too unstable. There's too much animosity. She will die.'

'I promise you, I'm on it,' the Doctor assured her. 'So, Yewans are not born, they are reincarnated. Same DNA. The ancestors have the same DNA, maybe. Possibly. What is the orb?'

'It holds the collective soul of the ancestors,' Ruby told him.

'I knew it. Maybe we can reconnect them, stabilise them. Kubuntu and her children, even just for a moment.' The Doctor inspected the life-sized onyx statue, his eyes narrowing on the carved handprints on her palms. He turned to Mya, who was still cradling Nazari. 'Please trust me,' he said gently, meeting resistance as he tried to lift Nazari. 'I promise, just two seconds.' Reluctantly, Mya conceded and walked over to the statue. The Doctor showed her what to do, placing her hand in Kubuntu's and wrapping her thumb around the back.

'Ah, the hand hug,' the Doctor murmured, a hint of a smile on his face as he executed the manoeuvre. 'Stay there, use your connection. Think good thoughts, happy thoughts.' Mya looked at Nazari and allowed a smile to sneak onto her face. Her tattoos gleamed and the flickering orb stabilised.

Suddenly, panels shot out from the sides of the statue, revealing buttons and switches reminiscent of the systems the Doctor had seen in the security base. The chest of the statue transformed into a monitor, its glow casting eerie shadows. In the distance, the sound of laser fire began again, a stark reminder of the chaos outside.

Nazari shot awake, hyperventilating as she struggled to regulate her breathing. Mya let go of the statue to console her, but the orb's shaking intensified, emitting beams of light that took form and materialised into Light Wraiths. As the spectral beings flew around, a tortured song filled the air. Tears began to roll down Mya and Nazari's faces.

Mya quickly replaced her hand on the statue, but nothing changed. Desperation flashed in her eyes as she wiped away the salty sting from them. Nazari struggled to her feet. With determination, she grabbed the other hand of Kubuntu's statue. Their eyes met, and they exchanged a hopeful smile. Their tattoos glowed brightly, illuminating the space around them.

The Light Wraiths ceased their wailing and froze, suspended in the air like ghostly apparitions held in a moment of time.

'Something ain't adding up, Ruby babes,' the Doctor said. 'In fact, nothing is adding up, which is even more mad. You see, this is different, much more advanced than the other security base, because this is the O.G. – the original. Sleek cos it's sentient. Not much need for buttons and widgets cos it's a living thing and the other is manmade, probably built with the resort 200 years ago.'

'By whom?' Mya interjected frustratedly.

'Oh! I'm getting it…' The Doctor's mind was turning. His fingers glided across the face of the panel, pressing a button and flicking a single switch. 'Initiating a total lockdown in the inner sanctum,' he said with a casual swagger. He flicked a switch, and stasis fields shone from the Light Wraiths, catching everyone in their light, dragging them from all over the inner sanctum and back towards the statue.

He looked up and saw Lori, Bia Toh, Bia Tatu, Fala, Fran and the Bia vigilantes, all suspended slightly above the ground, frozen in their attitudes by the stasis field like some surreal painting.

'If we're all sitting comfortably, then I'll begin,' said the Doctor. 'So many questions, so many thoughts and feelings, so much noise that I couldn't work it out. My first question: how is everyone getting in and out without so much as a ping on the security systems?' He pointed the security relay upwards and it projected the screen holographically for all to see. 'At first glance, the systems have two primary levels of security – the regular shmegular defences and the Wraith systems. But if you're super clever like me, you can see behind all that is a *third* telepathic defence mechanism.'

'What are you talking about, Doctor?' Mya said. 'That's impossible.'

'Yes, because there is a biometrical lock which means only Admin can tamper with the systems. So they are the only ones who could teleport people in and out.' He turned to face Mya. 'Isn't that, right?'

Mya frowned. 'If you are insinuating what I think you are—'

'I mean, you and I were the only ones in the security room when Fran got in. You're the only one with access.'

'I could say the same of you, Doctor,' Mya returned with the same level of recrimination. 'I didn't even know this security panel existed. No one has been in and amongst the ancestors in years.'

The Doctor smiled. 'A friendly Wraith passed through me earlier and left a subconscious note in my head. Did almost kill me in the process but I figure it was just trying to wake me up – because of all the noise I couldn't quite figure it out. The Wraiths, the Orb, you, you're all connected. Kubuntu must have made you all from the same thing.'

'So there's a world in which the Wraiths are like ghosts of past heirs and Keepers?' suggested Ruby.

The Doctor snapped his fingers. 'Oh, that's good!' He looked at Mya apologetically. 'Of course it's not Mya letting people come and go. Sorry, still processing.' He turned to Fran. 'Who let you in? Why do you think Bia Can and Bia Toh killed your brother?'

The Wraith alarms blared again, louder than they ever had before, and a black mist seeped into the atmosphere from thin air.

'Not today, thank you.' The Doctor tapped a button and shut them off.

Ruby clutched her stomach, looking relieved. 'How'd you do that?'

'*Those* Wraiths are impostors. Fakes controlled by the resort systems, which were built only 200 years ago,' the Doctor said. 'Now I've got access to the real deal, I overrode the alarm. Fran, you were saying?'

He pressed a few buttons and released Fran from the stasis field. Dropping to the ground with a small bump, Fran stood up slowly, took a deep breath and began. 'After you sent me and the other Bia away, my friends reassured me they had a way back in. A man on the inside. I never saw his face; he wore a mask.'

'Same as the guy who let me and Fala in!' Ruby interjected excitedly. 'Sorry.'

Fran continued: 'Famine had ravaged Bia. For almost two centuries now, our people have been eating food from replicators. Nothing fresh. We were dying faster than we could repopulate. Then the replicators started to malfunction, and we didn't have the minerals to fix them. We cried out, over and over, to the Bia High Court, but our prayers were ignored.'

'You lie!' Bia Toh snapped, struggling against the stasis field that still held him entrapped. 'We have heard no prayers. We've only been here a couple of years …'

'It's been 199 years!' Fran retorted. 'This High Court left before I was even born! I am a child of the famine.'

A stunned silence passed over the gathered crowd. The Doctor looked at the dumbfounded Bia nobles; they genuinely hadn't known.

'They arrived just after the last recorded Ijoa; they couldn't have known about the famine or what they were walking into,' the Doctor reasoned with Fran.

'I read about the Ijoa and figured: you must have come here and just never come back. Now I see why … life is cushy here,' Fran said through pained, gritted teeth.

'So you went undercover. I suppose your tattoos haven't healed properly,' the Doctor said empathetically.

'I sculpted them myself,' Fran said, his voice trembling. 'I had to bring them back, to get them to help and answer to their people. This place was so massive, and I could never get close enough to the Court. I knew I had to cover more ground. I sent for my brother and he brought friends,' he said, indicating the Bia vigilantes who hadn't moved a muscle in the last few minutes. 'But when they arrived, he was so sick. He didn't last a week. He died because they abandoned us.' Fran sobbed violently, struggling to get his words out.

Bia Toh exclaimed again, clearly tired of the accusations. 'No prayers were sent to us. No actions required of us.'

'And there it is! The third layer of security!' sighed the Doctor, his voice tinged with frustration and relief. 'I felt it before but couldn't access it. It's a psychotelepathic shield!'

'A shield? You mean it's been blocking our people's prayers?' Bia Tatu asked, his voice quivering.

'Poor Bia,' the Doctor said sympathetically. 'All those telepathic cries for help never making it through.'

'It's like the gods have switched off their data roaming,' Ruby said, shaking her head.

'This is impossible,' Bia Toh declared. 'How could this happen?'

Mya, looking pale, unconsciously let go of Kubuntu's hand. 'You think this shield was generated by the Garden, Doctor?'

'Hold on, there's something I don't get,' Ruby said, frowning. 'Why haven't you got a bone to pick with Prince Lori?'

'I dunno, maybe he's a figurehead. Practically decoration. No offence, Your Highness,' Fran said apologetically. 'I just can't seem to care about him.'

Lori stared into space, avoiding eye contact with everyone present apart from Fala.

Just then, the stasis fields trapping them shattered, and they all thumped to the ground. Everything happened in an instant. Fala fired at the Bia vigilante, who immediately returned fire.

'What the hell are you doing?' the Doctor cried, lifting his eyes to see fifteen Firebrand insurgents advancing through a tall flowerbed. Dark shrouded Wraiths rose from the brook and took out some of them, absorbing them into their forms. *No gold accents*, the Doctor noted. Amid the ensuing chaos, the Light Wraiths formed a protective barrier around Ruby, the Doctor, Nazari and Mya.

Ruby gazed around in horror. 'Plan's going great, then?' she said sarcastically, looking back at the Doctor and raising two ironic thumbs.

'Oh, I'm an idiot. Two thumbs up!' the Doctor whooped. 'Two thumbs UP!' He turned to Mya and Nazari. 'The psionic bond needs to be broken. The systems will respond better to you. You have to break it. Channel all your energy into thinking... freedom, liberation... Anything. But. This.'

Nazari and Mya focused intensely, their forms glowing brighter and brighter until the light became blinding. Suddenly, a bright white light blasted through the systems.

'You absolutely smashed it!' yelled the Doctor, but his words were lost as a tsunami of whisperings crashed over the room. Forgotten prayers built and built, overlapping and thrashing like living things begging and pleading. So much pain. So much anguish. Beneath all the words, the sounds of children screaming and mothers crying filled the Doctor's head, burning behind his eyes. He saw Ruby clutching her temples, screaming silently. He took hold of her and layered his hands on top of hers. Everyone else clutched their heads just before they all fell unconscious.

Eleven

Ruby looked around. 'What happened?' she asked weakly.

'The psionic impact of centuries of backed-up prayers, amplified by the crystals, short-circuited everyone for a minute,' the Doctor explained. 'Lucky for us, I'm used to that many voices in my head.'

Bia Toh recovered next and helped Fran to his feet. 'I'm sorry. We have neglected our duties, but I thank you for giving our lives purpose again. I assure you I didn't know. Or maybe I did know but didn't care. But I will make sure we return at once. This won't make up for the loss of your brother or his friends…' He stopped in his tracks; the masked men had gone. 'Where did they go?'

Fran looked around, searching for the vigilantes, but there was no trace of them.

Fala came to and immediately grabbed a weapon. She pointed it at Bia Tatu, who raised his hands in surrender.

'We are leaving,' he said. 'We have heard, and we are leaving. There is no need for this.'

'I don't care! Mya, they'll come back; you know they will. Look what they did to Nazari, to our sacred ground. They attacked her in the street. They…' She trailed off desperately as she could see Mya wasn't taking the bait.

'Doctor, could you lower the defences?' Bia Toh requested. 'We will be leaving now.'

'You can't... Can they, Your Highness?' The Doctor turned to face Lori.

'What?' Lori asked, snapping out of his trance but clearly feigning ignorance.

'It took me a while to figure it out,' said the Doctor. 'I blame the voices. Actually, I think I did know but for obvious reasons didn't care. It's you. This is all you.'

Lori chuckled incredulously and then stopped promptly upon realising that the Doctor was completely serious. 'Who, me? How?'

The Doctor stepped towards him. 'At every step, there was a distraction, a question. Every piece of the impossible puzzle I put together, you'd mix in a totally different jigsaw or just flip the table completely.' He looked around to find confused faces amongst the group. 'Sorry, that's a metaphor I came up with in my head, just realising you weren't a part of it. It's a whole thing... you had to be there.' He turned swiftly back to Lori, who still wore his unassuming smile. 'You've been there at every step. In the market, at the festival. It's all you.'

'What are you talking about, Doctor?' Ruby asked.

The Doctor walked towards Lori. 'Look around. Go on, look. Where is everyone? At points it seemed like there were scores of Firebrand and tens of Bia and now...'

Ruby looked around the room. No Dark Wraiths, no vigilantes. Just Lori, Fala and the original two

Firebrand members, Bia Tatu, Bia Toh, Fran, Mya, Nazari and the Doctor.

'Inconsistencies everywhere and they all link back to you.' The Doctor gazed at Lori, a smile playing on his lips. 'I spy with my little eye ... something beginning with ... M for moonstone!'

Lori's incredulous smile began to crumble. 'You've gone mad.'

The Doctor leapt at him and wrestled the moonstone ring off his finger. He took the tiny crystal out and held it up in the air. 'You've been lurking here among the spirits of the ancestors for a long time, haven't you? Absorbing them, hiding in the Gardens, insinuating yourself into the systems. Posing as a *Dark* Wraith, because you can't imitate a soul.'

The Doctor stepped back and watched as Lori began to sweat. The prince staggered to his feet and lunged at the Doctor, who sidestepped him and threw the crystal at Kubuntu's statue, directly at the spot of the missing jewel.

'Doctor, what is going on?' Mya asked.

'The first time Lori met Ruby was in the hotel room. How did he know what a thumbs-up was? No one else knew. Mya, you looked at him like he was an alien. He said he'd seen Ruby do it before. How?' The Doctor waited for a moment; Lori began to shake and glitch. 'Because he had seen it before, just not through his eyes.' He turned to face Fala, who smiled and collapsed in on herself. Mya gasped and ran to what was left of her sister.

Lori stumbled again. 'Oh, Doctor, you couldn't just leave it alone. You can never just leave it alone. Drink the water and keep forgetting.'

Mya gasped again; she looked as if she had seen a ghost. Standing where Lori had been was Fala. With every menacing step towards the Doctor, 'Lori' glitched again, becoming all three masked Bia vigilantes, then Bia Chey and then Mo.

'How is that possible?' Nazari stepped back, knocked off balance by shock.

'When Bia and Yewans die, they turn to crystal,' the Doctor said, hoping that would get the gears working in his audience's brains.

'This lot collapsed in on themselves!' Ruby realised.

'You, Ruby Sunday, are switched on!' The Doctor turned back to Lori and, for the first time in a long while, there wasn't a hint of amusement or intrigue on his face. 'Who are you? Who are you really?'

Lori continued to flicker through different forms: a Dark Wraith, Mo again and then back to Fala.

'Oh, honey, this is getting old,' said the Doctor. 'Pick one and stick to it, you're making me nauseous.'

Lori stopped as an ungodly amalgamation of all he had been, a Frankenstein's monster-type creature. Lori's face, with the torso of a Wraith, the legs of three Bia and the voice of them all. 'Our name has faded into nothing. You and I are very alike, Doctor. Nameless... But I saw into Ruby Sunday's soul and I saw myself in her mind and yours, Doctor. A word so sweet that billions have burnt in its name...'

'Come on now, get on with it,' the Doctor said, snapping his fingers impatiently.

EMPIRE.

The word settled telepathically in the consciouses of all present. It sent a painful shiver down Ruby's spine.

The Doctor smiled. 'Ah, a gestalt entity that can generate several forms at once, amplified by the crystal in the ring. But I bet now you are absolutely losing it.'

Out of the amalgamation of beings, Empire began to split again. Out from its body, one by one, replicas of Bia vigilantes, Firebrand members and Wraiths formed a small army behind Lori.

'We were once the original native life form of Yewa. Kubuntu made us first! We were born out of dust and dirt, and she deemed us a mistake,' Lori hissed.

'Like a pancake, the first one always comes out a bit rubbish,' the Doctor joked. 'Not the time... sorry.'

'Then she made the Yewa and the Bia out of her light and crystal form and deemed the Yewa and the Bia perfect.' He pointed at the orb. 'She loved them, nurtured them. Kubuntu left us to wither but we did not die! The anger we felt, the frustration and resentment, it fuelled us... united us.'

'It became you,' said the Doctor quietly.

'We fed on it. Fed on each other, until there was nothing left. And then we absorbed each other and became many in one. We then tried to feed off the dissent of the ancestors, their frustration, but there was so little. When they let the Bia build the resort, there was enough difference to build resentment, and the resentment was enough for us to grow stronger. But we needed more. Empire needed more. So we devised a plan. We would become them all.'

'So you've been sat here like a spider gorging itself on every fly around,' said the Doctor. 'Manipulating all sides – taking different forms in order to set everyone at each other's throats, controlling the defences, killing innocent people.'

Empire shifted from Lori and became Nazari. 'Yes, and now it is time to unleash maximum conflict.' It had taken her likeness but couldn't quite grasp her melodic voice; its impersonation was too rough and had echoes of Lori beneath it. 'We will raze this garden to the ground and absorb you all. I planned to use this place as an all-you-can-eat buffet but this game, this narrative, is getting boring. Maybe I will start a war with the Bia in the name of our loss and then use my power to spread and conquer new worlds. A true Empire! And I might just start with Earth.' Empire laughed and with each cackle they flicked between Lori and Nazari.

Nazari – the real Nazari – started towards him but was held back by Mya. 'You dare use my likeness for such sacrilege! I swear by the ancestors I will—'

'Where is my sister?' Mya demanded. 'Where is Fala?'

'Oh, Fala. I met her in a dingy part of the market. She had figured out something was wrong with the water supply and gathered a band of environmental lunatics to filter out my special ingredients. I consumed her and took her form. It didn't take long to pivot the mission of the Firebrand to my personal agenda. I absorbed her, as I did her ancestors.' Empire closed its eyes as if overwhelmed with happiness. 'Their resentment was so sweet, I couldn't get enough. Usually I have some self-control – I can't keep feeding if they're dead – but oh... so sweet.' Empire shrugged. 'Besides, I couldn't have doppelgängers walking about.'

A fury rose in Mya, so white hot, it paralysed her, such that all she could do was cry silently.

Empire inhaled and stabilised as Lori for a moment.

'It's feeding, Mya,' said the Doctor. 'I am so sorry. I understand your rage, I really, really get it, but Empire's feeding off that anger. It'll absorb you if you give into all that hate.' The Doctor turned back to Lori. 'That's why you can sustain their forms. They're a part of you.'

'Where is Prince Lori?' Bia Tatu chimed in. 'You – I mean, he left with us.'

'Oh, he was the sweetest, he had so much hope left in him. He had been reading and learning, and he hated that the Bia had been taking advantage of the Yewan people. He wanted to make a change. He wanted to help his people without exploiting the Yewa. Big plans to destroy the resort.' Empire's many forms licked their fingers as they shifted, as each pointed at the moonstone that once sat on his finger. 'I couldn't have that. This place was a symbol of oppression, and I needed to feed.'

'You're sick,' Ruby said.

'We are *inexorable*,' Empire replied.

'No, I mean, you look sick.'

They really did, all of them. The entire army looked feverish – sweaty and feeble. Fala's depiction was shaking, Mo had fallen to his knees and the multiple Bia vigilantes and Firebrand members were writhing in pain. 'I need that moonstone back,' they said with a collective breathless menace.

'You know, the thing about empires is that they all fall in the end,' the Doctor said. 'And you've messed up. You've given a group of telepathic beings a common enemy and a shared goal in the most powerful amplifier of energy in the known universe.' He clapped his hands. 'People work best when they work together. Unity is so much more powerful than fear or dissent. And without that moonstone to harness your power, I reckon your days are numbered.'

Empire's manifestations, in unison, looked down at their shaking hands.

'It was you,' Nazari said. 'The ancestor showed us. You stole the moonstone, then posed as Bia and massacred reincarnation after reincarnation. You inflicted so much pain that the Ijoas were forced to stop. Memory became a strange thing over the generations; all our people recalled was the pain, and they didn't want to relive it. No one could remember what you had done.'

'But for the Bia, Empire needed a different approach,' the Doctor said. 'It made the Bia drink water laced with a potent potion from the Ratehs river. This made them so apathetic that even if they did see something or had an inkling of the truth, they wouldn't care. It made it easier for them to forget. Empire, you created discomfort to feed off their pain, and now it's poisoning your food supply because all the Bia and the Yewa are connected. You've absorbed part of them. Part of them lives in you, and if they can access that and bring light and unity, then ...'

One by one, the members of the army were reabsorbed into the Dark Wraith form. A mist grew out of Empire and grabbed the Doctor by the neck.

'You became a Wraith to distract me every time I got close to an answer.' The Doctor gasped. 'Making sly comments to keep Nazari and Mya apart because you knew their love was so strong it would consume you in seconds.' He gave a knowing wink to Mya and Nazari.

Empire now stood alone, a towering figure of darkness, with the Doctor captive under its arm, squeezing his neck, choking him. Empire's mist reached out and grabbed Bia Chey, Bia Tatu, Ruby and then Fran, one by one. Their screams filled the air as Empire began absorbing their life forces, sucking them into its shadowy form. Their bodies went limp and lifeless as they were pulled into the darkness, merging with the evil entity.

The sinister creature then turned its gaze towards Mya and Nazari, who stood a short distance away, protected by the radiant glow of the ancestors.

Empire moved towards them with a menacing slowness, savouring the fear it could sense emanating from them. The Doctor, still held captive, could feel Empire absorbing every negative emotion he had ever felt – anger, despair, guilt. The creature thrived on this negativity, growing stronger with each passing moment.

The ancestors, flickering like candles in a storm, fought valiantly to shield Nazari and Mya, but their energy was waning. In a desperate attempt to strengthen their defences, Nazari grabbed Mya's hand, hoping to feed more power to the ancient relic.

But it wasn't enough.

In a moment of clarity, Nazari and Mya turned to each other. Mya took a deep breath and leant in to kiss her. An intense light burst forth from their connection, causing the Light Wraiths to multiply and intensify. This newfound energy surged forward, attacking the Dark Wraith form of Empire with renewed vigour. Holes began to appear in its shadowy figure as the light pierced through.

Empire howled in agony, its grip on the Doctor and the others loosening.

'Yes!' the Doctor bellowed, as the dark entity released him and Ruby and the others. Their bodies fell to the ground as Empire began to shrink.

The onslaught of light continued unabated, tearing through the darkness until Empire was reduced to a mere speck. The Light Wraiths surrounded the speck, containing it and preventing it from regaining its strength.

The speck hung suspended in light.

And its final, pitiful scream rang on and on.

Twelve

Tangled in countless wires, sonic screwdriver between his teeth and the security relay in his hands, the Doctor was tinkering away at Mya's screen.

'What are you doing?' Ruby asked, from her perched position on the foyer's front desk.

Before he could respond, Bia Toh and the remains of the High Court appeared with their luggage. Fran shuffled along behind them. He looked ravaged by guilt, held up only by the strength of Bia Tatu.

'Thank you, Doctor,' Bia Toh said. 'I still have a slight headache because of you – these prayers are still coming through and lack of use has caused my brain to atrophy – definitely not as strong as it once was – but I am grateful to once again be of service to my people. There is much work to be done on Bia. We must hurry back.'

'Pleasure is all mine,' the Doctor replied. 'Oh, and hers,' he added, as Mya stepped out from the glass elevator with Nazari. 'The resort systems were built a century before you came. Those backed-up prayers were sitting in the void inside the psychotelepathic field for ages.'

'It's coming back to me,' Bia Toh told him. 'Bia Chey, Bia Ugon and Lori left Bia first; myself and Tatu had work to complete.' Bia Tatu had once again taken on his stoic silent vibe and simply nodded in agreement.

'They must have been consumed by Empire before you arrived,' said the Doctor. 'We're sorry for your loss.'

Bia Toh nodded sadly. 'We must take accountability. We are not too different from Empire. Before we came, we knew we would luxuriate at the expense of our sister planet. We cannot solely blame the Ratehs river for our lack of care. We have taken from them. It has always been the way, but no more. We owe a debt we can never really repay. But that doesn't mean we won't try.'

'What about Empire?' Fran asked.

'We will leave him in the Garden. Kubuntu's descendants have him covered now that the truth is out,' said Mya. 'Peace will flow, and he will be unable to feed.'

'Thank you, Doctor,' Nazari said. She turned to Bia Toh and stretched her palm to his. He looked down at it, then raised his own. They wrapped their thumbs around each other's and smiled.

'Thank you for your hospitality, Nazari, heir of Kubuntu, and Mya, Keeper of her Gardens. It was our pleasure to be your honoured guests. We will now return to Bia and bother you no longer.'

Nazari stepped back to stand next to Mya once again. 'Bia Toh, you will always be welcome here. I realised I never met the real Lori; he sounded wonderful. His memory will always be honoured here. Please return to us if you need anything.'

Bia Toh nodded and stretched his hand to Fran. With that, the Bia exited the Gardens through the foyer.

Ruby slid off Mya's desk. 'So, what's up for you two now?' she asked with an air of insinuation that caught the Doctor's attention. He stopped tinkering and stood up as straight as the tangled wires would allow, waiting for a response.

Mya smiled. 'We will continue Kubuntu's good work. We will replant throughout the city and dismantle the spa crystal by crystal.'

Ruby had meant more relationship-wise, but figured that, with all that had happened, romance wasn't really on the cards right now. Still, they were gleaming, their tattoos holding a warm, steady glow. She glanced down to find Mya's pinky finger wrapped around Nazari's, and it tasted like vanilla and cinnamon.

'Right, I've dismantled the resort systems,' the Doctor said, untangling himself from the mess of wires.

As he spoke, Light Wraiths rose from the floor and shimmered around them, their ethereal forms pulsing with newfound freedom.

'The physical manifestations of your ancestors are no longer confined to the Gardens,' the Doctor went on. 'The Bia building the hotel, and the Empire consuming them, posing as them, they must have felt like they couldn't leave. Staying to fight against their impostors. Now, liberated, they can walk among the people of Yewa as they once did.'

Ruby watched as the Wraiths moved through the air, dispersing towards the city. A sense of peace settled over her. The ancestors' presence symbolised a new dawn for the Yewa people, one where the past's pain could be transformed into a source of strength and unity.

'We honestly cannot thank you both enough,' Nazari said. 'We would love to offer you our premium room before we tear down the resort and return the Gardens to their primary function.'

The Doctor and Ruby turned to look at each other and spoke in unison.

'Hell, yeah!'

An hour later, in the wave pool of the premium suite, the Doctor splashed around with an assortment of inflatable toys modelled after various animals native to Yewa: a snow chicken, a polar dog and an arctic giraffe. He climbed out of the pool to sit beside Ruby, who was sunbathing under the skylight.

They exhaled, a simultaneous sigh of relief. A few moments of blissful silence passed; nothing was said but everything felt understood. Eventually…

'Doctor…'

'Ruby…'

'I'm bored.'

'Thank heavens. Quick as you can, get packed. There's a nebula in the Kratarian District that is apparently being stalked by cyber-ghosts.'

The two friends jumped to their feet and began packing their stuff.

'I just don't think I'm a holiday person,' Ruby said as she made a beeline for one of the bathrooms.

'You're telling me. I have the worst luck with them. Orphan 55? A mess. Paradise Towers? Stressful! And don't even get me started on Midnight …' He shuddered. 'Echoes still give me the heebie-jeebies. Never trust a crystalline planet to not have weird stuff going on.'

He walked into the bathroom to find Ruby stuffing all the toiletries into his clutch. Towels, soaps, moisturisers and shampoos.

'Ruby Sunday!' The Doctor put on a face of pantomime concern. 'What are you doing?'

She stopped and looked up at him. 'Come on, Doctor. Who doesn't help themselves to the hotel freebies? Specially when you save the hotel and a couple of planets into the bargain.'

The Doctor grinned. 'You have a point!' He started packing whatever he could into his pockets.

'There is just one thing I don't get,' said Ruby. 'Empire could have killed me at so many points. What was it waiting for?'

'There is a thin line between fear and violence. What does a wounded animal do? Snarl. You see a scary spider and, although it's tiny, the first instinct for most people is "grab a slipper". Scared people do scary things. If your diet is dissent, what do you do?'

'Create fear.'

'*Exactement*, Ruby. Now, that fear, if left to mature, will become rage, and that rage will create violence, and that violence will create more violence, which will create more fear, *et voilà*: all-you-can-eat buffet.'

'Ooh.' Ruby clutched her stomach as it rumbled. 'Buffet?'

'You don't have to ask me twice.' The Doctor beamed. 'See, now, that's a diet I can get behind!'

Acknowledgements

Thank you to the indigenous peoples of Hawaii and Jamaica, who served as the original inspiration for this story. I pray you get your beaches back.

Although I did most of the heavy lifting myself, I am endlessly grateful to my endless community. To my friends, I hope you recognise the legacy of your love and friendship woven throughout this narrative. May you hear our catchphrases, see our mannerisms and laugh at the echoes of our cherished inside jokes.

A special shout-out to my muses: Effie, Cassiopeia, Taiwo and Faith. You are my daily reminder that love conquers all.

Also available from BBC Books

BBC DOCTOR WHO

CAGED

UNA McCORMACK

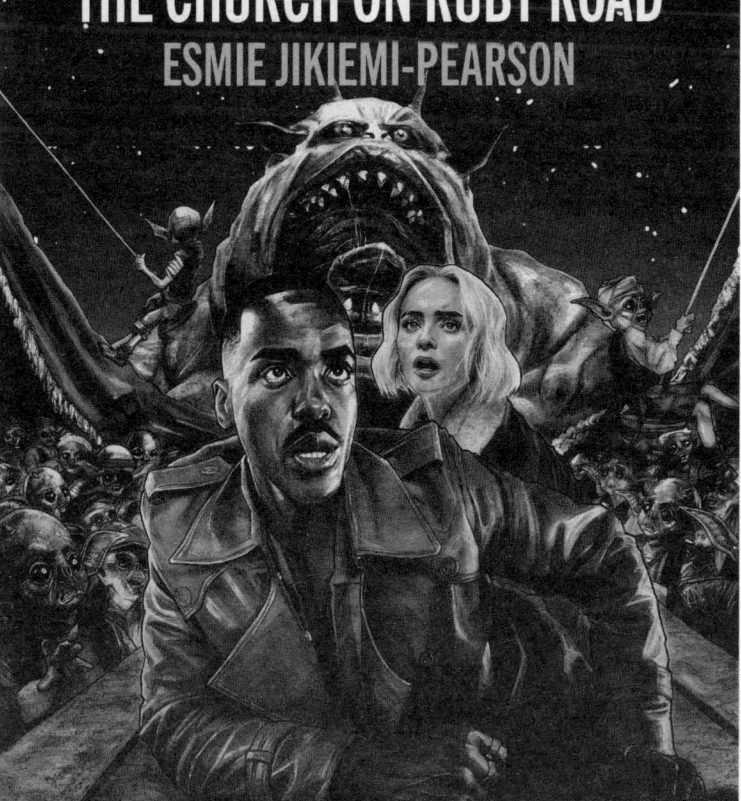

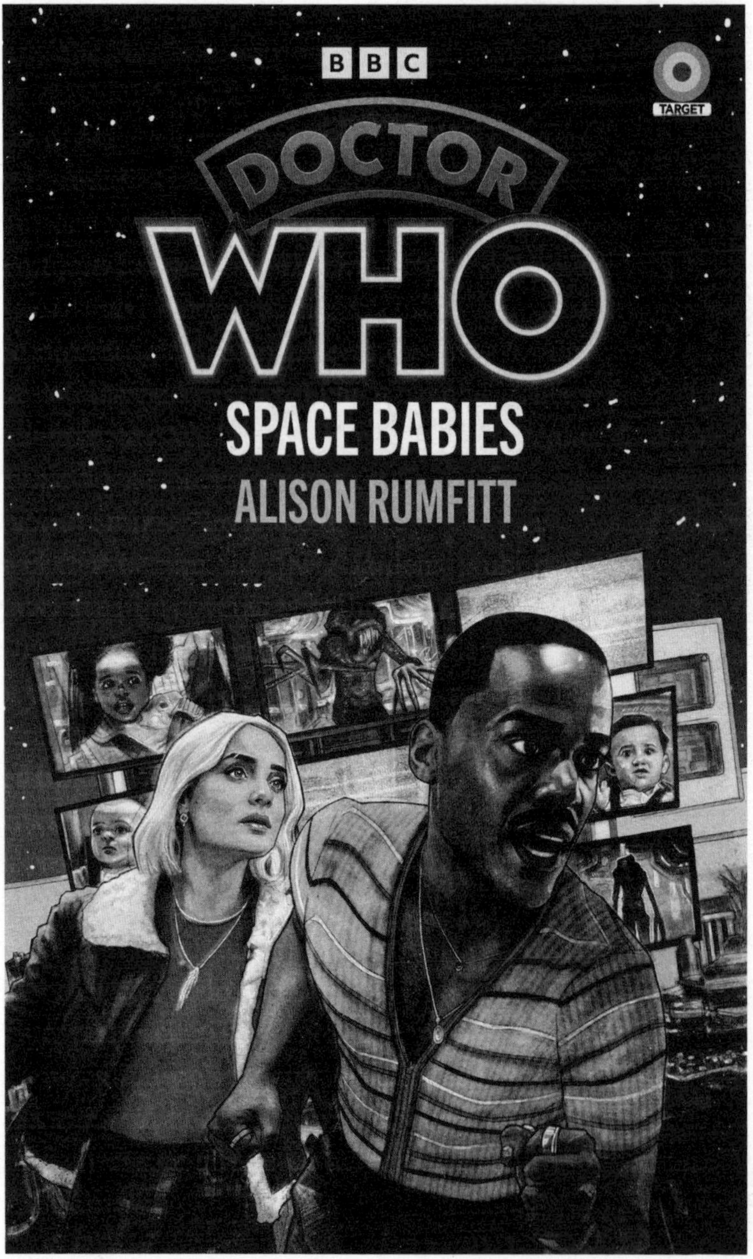
BBC
TARGET
DOCTOR
WHO
SPACE BABIES
ALISON RUMFITT

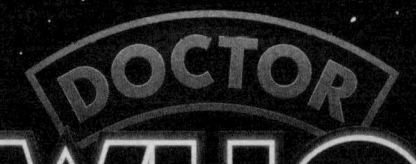

DOCTOR WHO

73 YARDS

SCOTT HANDCOCK

DOCTOR WHO

ROGUE

KATE HERRON & BRIONY REDMAN